W9-BGX-444

ALL DOUBTS DISPELLED

Any kind thoughts Emmaline might have had about Lord Jeremy Barnett vanished as he pulled her to him, and brought his arrogant lips down on hers. A gleam of amusement lit his eyes as he looked down at her flushed face.

"Like it, my dear?" he asked sardonically.

"Let me go or I'll scream!" Emmaline whispered.

Jeremy laughed. "Scream? And have the servants come running? I think not."

In despair, Emmaline knew he was right, and she once more tried to twist free. But Jeremy held her still, and again lowered his lips to hers, this time more slowly and gently, until, helplessly, she swayed toward him and her lips parted.

Her eyes were still shut, her body limp, her heart beating wildly, when he thrust her from him.

"Really," he mocked, "you must learn to restrain this wayward nature of yours before it lands you in the briars. . . ."

(For a list of other Signet Regency Romances by April Kihlstrom, please turn page. . . .)

Ø SIGNET REGENCY ROMANCE   (0451)

PROPER ALLIANCES,
IMPROPER PASSIONS

☐ THE BELEAGUERED LORD BOURNE by Michelle Kasey. (140443—$2.50)
☐ THE TOPLOFTY LORD THROPE by Michelle Kasey.   (145623—$2.50)
☐ NABOB'S WIDOW by April Kihlstrom.   (144368—$2.50)
☐ A COUNTERFEIT BETROTHAL by April Kihlstrom.   (140827—$2.50)
☐ THE CHARMING IMPOSTOR by April Kihlstrom.   (138023—$2.50)
☐ A SCANDALOUS BEQUEST by April Kihlstrom.   (138821—$2.50)
☐ A CHOICE OF COUSINS by April Kihlstrom.   (113470—$2.25)
☐ THE EARL'S INTRIGUE by Elizabeth Todd.   (128745—$2.25)
☐ LADY CHARLOTTE'S RUSE by Judith Harkness.   (143027—$2.50)
☐ CONTRARY COUSINS by Judith Harkness.   (110226—$2.25)
☐ THE DETERMINED BACHELOR by Judith Harkness.   (142608—$2.50)
☐ THE ADMIRAL'S DAUGHTER by Judith Harkness.   (138368—$2.50)

Prices slightly higher in Canada

Buy them at your local bookstore or use this convenient coupon for ordering.

NEW AMERICAN LIBRARY,
P.O. Box 999, Bergenfield, New Jersey 07621

Please send me the books I have checked above. I am enclosing $_____
(please add $1.00 to this order to cover postage and handling). Send check
or money order—no cash or C.O.D.'s. Prices and numbers subject to change
without notice.

Name _____

Address_____

City_____State_____Zip Code_____
               Allow 4-6 weeks for delivery.
        This offer is subject to withdrawal without notice.

The Counterfeit Betrothal

by
April Kihlstrom

A SIGNET BOOK

NEW AMERICAN LIBRARY

NAL BOOKS ARE AVAILABLE AT QUANTITY DISCOUNTS
WHEN USED TO PROMOTE PRODUCTS OR SERVICES.
FOR INFORMATION PLEASE WRITE TO PREMIUM MARKETING DIVISION,
NEW AMERICAN LIBRARY, 1633 BROADWAY,
NEW YORK, NEW YORK 10019.

Copyright © 1987 by April Kihlstrom

All rights reserved

SIGNET TRADEMARK REG. U.S. PAT. OFF. AND FOREIGN COUNTRIES
REGISTERED TRADEMARK—MARCA REGISTRADA
HECHO EN CHICAGO, U.S.A.

SIGNET, SIGNET CLASSIC, MENTOR, ONYX, PLUME, MERIDIAN
and NAL BOOKS are published by NAL PENGUIN INC.,
1633 Broadway, New York, New York 10019

First Printing, August, 1987

1 2 3 4 5 6 7 8 9

PRINTED IN THE UNITED STATES OF AMERICA

1

LORD Barnett stood at the window of his richly appointed library, his hands clasped behind his back as he watched with ill-concealed agitation for his son's carriage to appear. That the boy had been sent a summons meant little, he feared, unless Jeremy chose, for reasons of his own, to acknowledge it. This somber reflection led the baron to sigh and wish, not for the first time, that his wife had lived. Or that he had had the resolution to remarry at some point in the past twenty-eight years so that someone might have taken Jeremy in hand and exerted a calming influence upon the boy.

Gilbert Barnett was sufficiently vain to feel that he would have had no difficulty in finding someone suitable to become the second Lady Barnett. In this case vanity coincided with reality. Even now, at fifty-two, Barnett was a remarkably handsome man. He was, moreover, in excellent health and had the prospect of a good many years ahead of him if family tradition held true. Indeed, Barnett's own physician had once jokingly suggested that the Barnetts obviously had access to the *elixir vitae*.

As if an aristocratic heritage and a prepossessing appearance were not enough, Gilbert also was the owner of an extremely large estate. The Barnetts had combined financial prudence with advantageous marriages to produce an ever-increasing family fortune. There had never been a rake in the family. At least not until Jeremy, Lord Barnett's son. Previous Barnetts had been content with quiet existences in the countryside except for the occasional ventures to London, particularly for the purpose of finding a wife, and Gilbert had even managed to avoid that, marrying his childhood sweetheart from one of the neighboring estates.

Jeremy, on the other hand, had, at his own request been sent off to school at an early age to be educated and then, upon leaving Eton and being cashiered from Cambridge, gone straight to London, returning only when expressly summoned by his father. It was an arrangement that seemed to suit both men perfectly. Or had until now. Disquieting rumors about his son's activities were reaching Lord Barnett and in response he had issued his current command.

As he watched, Barnett saw his son's curricle come down the drive and he hastily moved away from the window. On no account did he wish Jeremy to know he had been watching for him. Instead he rang for the footman and gave orders—for perhaps the tenth time—concerning his son's arrival.

Jeremy Barnett found the occasion no less disquieting than Lord Barnett. He had long since ceased to look for affection from his father but he had not yet lost all hope of a grudging acceptance.

Some might have argued that the life he led was quite certain to ensure the direct opposite but logic was not what drove Jeremy Barnett. What drove him was a lifetime of alternating inattention and blame from his father for having been born on the precise day that his mother had died. At eight and twenty Jeremy Barnett appeared every inch the hardened rake, particularly when he stood, as now, on ancestral ground.

Hargraves, who opened the door to him, was delighted to see young Barnett. "Master Jeremy," he said in a tone of intense gratification, "how pleasant to see you, sir. And may I say that you look very fine in that coat?"

Jeremy smiled unabashedly as he handed over the coat with its capes to Hargraves, not minding in the least the liberty taken by this old family retainer. The servants at Barnett Hall had always seemed more his family than his own father. "How are you, Hargraves?" he demanded. "You look as healthy as ever! And how is Mrs. Hargraves?"

"Anxious to see you again, sir," the butler answered with a smile of his own. "As is his lordship. P'rhaps I'd best take you to the library straight away."

"In the devil of a mood, is he?" Jeremy asked lightly.

Hargraves coughed. "As to that, I believe more than I have ever known him to be. I should step warily, Master Jeremy. He has been looking like thunder itself these past two weeks."

Those words abruptly enlightened young Barnett. "Heard about the incident at Covent Gardens, has he?" Jeremy said, more to himself than to anyone else. He managed, nevertheless, to clap

Hargraves on the shoulder and reassure him lightly, "I shall come about, Hargraves, I always do."

Jeremy paused at the doorway. He had always hated this room, with its dark furniture and bookcases and heavy blue velvet curtains. It was too much his father's room for him to ever feel at ease there, though he dearly loved to read. Unconsciously Jeremy squared his shoulders and reminded himself that he had never yet failed somehow to placate his father. Upon entering the library, however, and seeing his father's face, Jeremy found he was no longer so certain that he would be able to do so this time. Both men stood looking at one another. They were in such marked contrast in their dress that had the family features not been stamped so prominently upon both faces one might have wondered if they were strangers.

Each eyed the other with something akin to distaste. Lord Barnett wore the comfortable clothes of a country gentlemen. Jeremy wore yellow pantaloons that might have been molded to his figure at the same time as the brown coat of superfine. The boots were polished and the neckcloth tied with the skill of one who had spent many hours in practice. And his hair was curled and scented while a superflous quizzing glass dangled from a velvet ribbon around his neck. Gilbert snorted in disgust.

Jeremy bowed ironically. "How distressed I am, Father, that my attire is not to your liking. I am desolate."

Angrily Gilbert waved his son to a chair. "Have done with your nonsense," he said. "I've no mind for it today. You only confirm me in my decision."

"And what decision is that, pray tell, Father?" Jeremy asked in a mincing voice that would have

gone unrecognized by any of his London acquaint-
ances.

"That you must be married at once," the elder
Barnett retorted.

For a moment there was absolute silence in the
room. When Jeremy spoke again, his voice was
dangerously quiet as he said, "Have I mistaken
you, Father, or did you say that you have decided
I must be married at once?"

"You heard me, right enough," Gilbert replied
briskly. "I had not meant to come to the point so
bluntly but as I have, I shall not back down."

"And have you, er, chosen my bride as well?"
Jeremy asked, looking at his impeccably manicured nails.

"I have. But I am perfectly willing to listen
should you wish to propose some other young
lady instead. Provided, of course, that she is of
good family and good reputation," Lord Barnett
said generously.

Jeremy's gaze became fixed upon his boots. In a
thoughtful voice he said, "Odd, I had not realized
I was breeding, or that any female of my most
intimate acquaintance was in the family way. Nor
have I compromised any gently bred ladies of late.
Therefore I fail to see why I *must* be married
immediately."

"This is not a matter for jesting!" Gilbert thundered as his fist slammed the desk before him.

"I did not think it was," Jeremy replied curtly. "I
repeat, I fail to see why I must be married at
once."

"Because if not, I shall cut you off without a
penny," Lord Barnett replied, speaking each word
quite distinctly.

Jeremy's eyebrows rose but his voice was steady as he said, "Disinherit me, Father? I had not thought the estate allowed it."

Barnett's lips twitched. "No, you know very well I cannot disinherit you," he said more calmly. "But my death is most likely a good many years away. At least I intend to take care to see that it is. No, I mean that should you refuse to obey my wishes in this matter I shall cut off your very generous allowance completely and you shall be cast upon your own resources until the day that I die. And since you have already run through the inheritance left by your mother, I think you shall not find that a very comfortable existence. Particularly as I shall also send word to the moneylenders of London that I shall be most angry if they lend you funds and shall pursue every legal possibility to tie up the estate so that you will be unable to repay them."

Now Jeremy did go very still. When he spoke, it was as though he was feeling his way. "What you propose amounts to either starvation or the despicable existence of depending upon charitable friends for every need until your existence is ended. Unless you have an alternative proposal such as buying me colors and allowing me to enter the military," he added. "Of course, I may be considered a trifle old for that but—"

Barnett shook his head. "That I shall never do. So I promised your mother before she died and so I shall keep my promise."

"Just because her brother died—"

"That is quite enough!" Barnett thundered. "The matter is not open to discussion. I shall keep my promise. What is open to discussion is your marriage. I have had reports of you from London that quite convince me I can no longer allow you free rein. Nor, it seems, can I control you myself. But perhaps a sensible marriage will serve to steady your nature, and at the very least it may provide an heir for the estate in the likely event you bring about your own demise in the very near future."

"I see. Covent Gardens?" Jeremy hazarded.

"Covent Gardens," Gilbert confirmed. "Though that is merely the latest in a long string of outrages. Well? I await your answer."

Parrying for time, Jeremy asked with a lightness he did not feel, "Am I permitted to ask who is this estimable female you have chosen for my bride-to-be?"

"Certainly," Lord Barnett replied, his normal color beginning to return. "I have in mind Emmaline Delwyn. Her family has known ours for years, and you have known her almost since her birth. The Delwyns are an excellent family and Emmaline herself a sensible, dutiful child. One cannot ask for better qualities in a wife."

Jeremy tried to summon up an image of the girl and could not. Although he had once known her well, that was some years ago and he could only recall that she seemed very young and very pert and something of a nuisance. It was her father he had usually gone to see. "How old is she now?" he asked mildly.

"Twenty."

"Twenty?" Jeremy sat up abruptly. "Good God, is she such an antidote that an excellent family and reasonable portion have not been sufficient to send her off?"

"Nothing of the sort," Barnett retorted angrily.

"While I do not say she is a beauty, she is certainly not disagreeable in her appearance. You would have nothing to be ashamed of in that respect. She has not been properly launched because she has spent the last several years nursing her father, who is ill. As you very well know. In any event, there has been no one to do it, as both her sisters married some years ago and her mother died of the ague shortly after that."

"I see. How comforting to be reassured as to her estimable qualities," Jeremy said sarcastically. "So I am to call upon this paragon of virtue and become betrothed to her in what length of time? A week? A month? Six months?"

"Not betrothed, married," the elder Barnett replied. "Her father is upon his deathbed and I should not like his death to come before you can be married. It would delay matters far too long."

"Of course," Jeremy agreed mockingly.

"You need not sneer," Gilbert said angrily. "I have not said you must marry Emmaline Delwyn. I am quite prepared to listen if you have any other names to put forward."

Jeremy waved a hand. "No, no, I've no one else to suggest. I do, however, have a question, Father. You have the means to compel me, or so you believe, to marry Miss Delwyn, but what in God's name makes you believe she will marry me?"

"She is a good girl and will do as her father tells her," Barnett said gruffly. "Sir Osbert is as anxious as I am to see his child settled, and he knows I can be counted upon to look after her if the two of you should marry."

Jeremy's eyes widened in astonishment. "Do you

mean to say, sir, that you have already discussed this with Sir Osbert?"

Barnett answered testily, "I have just said so, haven't I? Sir Osbert and I are old friends. It is he who mentioned his concern about Emmaline's future. Naturally it came to mind when I reached my decision that you must marry. We have not, however, spoken to the girl herself; that is up to you."

"How kind," Jeremy murmured.

"Now that is just what I will not tolerate!" Lord Barnett thundered. "If you do decide to offer for the girl you will do so with dignity and courtesy not with mocking humor. She is not to know the reason for the marriage and you are to be a proper husband to her."

"I am to pledge undying love, I suppose?" Jeremy countered.

"Of course not," Barnett replied. "That would be neither called for nor expected. Emmaline Delwyn is not some foolish chit who will expect nonsensical declarations of love. It is enough that she should suppose you wish to marry her because you have decided that she will make a suitable wife."

"I repeat, what if she will not have me?" Jeremy asked blandly.

"Should you decide to ask her," Barnett said levelly, "you will see to it that she does accept you. That should not be difficult if I am to credit half the tales of your charm with the ladies. But it is up to you. Marriage, to Emmaline Delwyn or any other young lady who meets with my approval, or you are cut off without a penny while I live. Which is it to be?"

"Since you stipulate that the young woman must meet with your approval, I have no alternative suggestion," Jeremy replied lazily. "Emmaline Delwyn I suppose it must be since I choose neither to starve nor to throw myself upon the mercy of my friends."

"What friends?" Lord Barnett snorted under his breath.

Jeremy ignored the interruption and went on, "I shall call upon Miss Delwyn the next time I am home. Right now I must be returning to London. I have pledged myself to be at a certain party tonight and—"

"And you are going nowhere," Lord Barnett cut short his son's excuses. "When you leave here, it is either as a married man or as a pauper. Until then you stay."

Jeremy Barnett fell back into the chair he had half risen from. "I see," he said grimly. "I shall give you my answer tomorrow after I have seen this vision of virtue you insist upon casting my way."

"Very well," Barnett said curtly. For a moment he hesitated, and when he spoke again his voice was softer and slightly tremulous. "You may not believe me when I say so, Jeremy, but I am thinking of your good when I propose this match. It may well be the making of you." Jeremy did not answer, however, and his father sighed. Then, consulting a clock on the mantelpiece above him, his lordship said, "You have scarcely enough time to dress for dinner if it takes you half the time it used to. You had best go upstairs at once."

With a bow, Jeremy Barnett did so.

2

SIR Osbert Delwyn had bought for his bride, some thirty years before, a neat little house in the Hampshire countryside near Selborne to which they had happily retreated, and over the years it had become a comfortable home. Its chief advantage, so far as Emmaline was concerned, was that it practically ran itself with little required on her part in the way of direction to the servants. The rooms were well cared for, the kitchen sufficiently modern to encourage excellent meals, and the situation presented pleasant views from almost every window. In happier days, the house had been noted for conviviality, and the Delwyns had been famous for their potluck suppers. When Emmaline's sisters had been courting, the house had frequently been filled with young men, and none had gone away complaining of a lack of hospitality—whatever their reception by the elder Miss Delwyns.

But it had been some years since the ring of laughter had filled the house. After Emmaline's mother had died, Sir Osbert had grown quieter and quieter and finally suffered a stroke that left him bedridden. His care had fallen upon Emmaline's shoulders since both her sisters had been caught up in motherhood. Emmaline had not complained then nor did she complain now, but it could not be denied that her thoughts often went to the London Season it seemed she would never have. To be sure, her sisters had not had such Seasons either, but they had each been wed scarcely a year out of the schoolroom and had made the choice themselves. For Emmaline the future seemed to stretch ahead with no prospect of change. The doctor said her father might die next week or linger on for years. Either way, in the end, Emmaline felt she faced only spinsterhood.

Still, it was not Emmaline's nature to dwell upon such things. In general she took each day as it came and tried to maintain her habitual cheerfulness, for it could not, as she frequently told Mrs. Bailey, the housekeeper, help her father to be forever surrounded by gloomy faces. And so she showed little discontent that the only regular visitors to the Delwyn house were Lord Barnett, the vicar, the doctor, and her two sisters. Of these her favorite was Lord Barnett because he could, at times, rouse her father to a vivacity that Emmaline remembered from the days before her mother died. He always looked, moreover, beyond the superficialities and seemed to grasp the intelligence in her fine brown eyes and to respect the strength of character that others were inclined to disparage as foolish stubborness.

On this particular morning Emmaline sat in the garden with both her sisters, who were competing with one another to describe the horrors their dear children had undergone with a recent bout of chicken pox. Emmaline could not help but send up a silent prayer of thanks that her duties as

nurse to her father had precluded being asked by
her sisters to come and nurse their darlings. Nor
could she help but contrast, with a pang of envy,
their fashionable dresses of brightly colored silk
with her own of practical checked muslin. Shining
dark hair in ringlets framed their faces while her
own chestnut locks, brushed neatly back, seemed
dull in comparison. It was not that Emmaline did
not care about her appearance, rather that the
duties that fell upon her shoulders precluded the
time needed to be so fashionable. And last night
had been a bad one for her father, and therefore
for Emmaline, who had to rise and go to his bedside
three or four times before dawn. Indeed, the doctor had said, upon his dawn visit, that while there
was no certainty in such matters, he despaired of
her father lasting out the year.

Jeremy Barnett, coming into the garden unan-
nounced, paused in the doorway to look at the
young woman who was supposed to become his
bride. With a pang he realized that the face he
had yesterday been unable to recall was suddenly
achingly familiar. How easily he now remembered
all the times Emmaline had come chasing at his
heels. Jeremy flushed, however, as he also recalled
the cool facade he had always adopted to prevent
her or anyone else from seeing how much he had
needed such adoration.

At Jeremy's shoulder Lord Barnett said quietly,
"You must not be thinking Miss Delwyn is a dowd.
Nothing of the sort! Generally, of course, she is
dressed quite practically for nursing her father, as
she is today. But I have seen her dressed as fine
as any London lady."

"Quite," Jeremy murmured ironically, playing the London fop to the last.

Contrary to his father's scornful belief, however, Jeremy did not think poorly of Emmaline. Her face was as graceful in repose as it had been mischievous in play years ago. Her eyes were clear, the nose delicate without being pert, and her mouth warm without being vulgar. Nor did his shrewd gaze miss the fact that her figure would, as the saying went, pay for the dressing. Indeed he was sure that given the opportunity, Emmaline would outshine her sisters with ease. Particularly when she smiled, as she did now at something her sister Caroline had said.

Barnett knew none of this, however. With a snort of anger at his son's apparent rudeness, he strode forward, calling out briskly, "Emmaline, my dear, how are you today? And your father? Ladies, how delightful to see you again."

Immediately, Emmaline was on her feet. "Lord Barnett, it is we who are delighted to see you. My father is eagerly awaiting your usual chess game."

"Is he indeed?" Barnett retorted. "Well, I vow I shall give the old rascal a run for his money! By the by, Emmaline, this is my rapscallion son, Jeremy. You must have met over the years and I trust you remember him?"

"Of course," Emmaline said with a friendly smile as she turned to the younger Barnett. With a pang of remembrance she noted his figure was as trim as ever and his clothes straight from the finest tailors in London. He was tall and handsome with dark brown hair she longed to touch—for her childish crush on Jeremy Barnett had given way to something more womanly. None of this betrayed itself as she said, "I've no doubt, however, that he has forgotten me. He is more likely to remember my sisters Caroline and Adeline."

Jeremy bowed to all three ladies, murmuring polite greetings as he did so. Up close he saw nothing to alter his earlier opinion. The two elder sisters had been well enough in their salad days, but motherhood had thickened their waists and sharpened their expressions. With a smile he bowed to Emmaline and said, "My father has told me something of your circumstances, Miss Delwyn, and I can only regret the cruel fate that has deprived us hereabouts of your lovely company at social affairs."

Emmaline regarded him shrewdly, her eyes twinkling slightly as she replied, "Come now, Mr. Barnett. I am not entirely a recluse, you must know. If we have not encountered one another socially, I suspect it is less from my seclusion than from your absence. We can scarcely compete, hereabouts, with the attractions of London."

Caroline and Adeline's eyebrows rose in surprised disapproval at the pertness of their sister's reply but Jeremy was not offended. He turned to his father and said, "I know you must be wanting to go upstairs and see Sir Osbert and so am I, though I shall be quite desolate to leave such lovely company as these three ladies afford. Adeline, Caroline, you seem not to have changed in the least over these past few years. I can scarcely believe you are matrons!"

Reassured at this evidence of his son's desire to be amiable, Lord Barnett flashed a final smile at Emmaline over his son's shoulder and said, "Well, then, I do confess an impatience to see Sir Osbert.

No need to take me up, Emmaline, I know my way well enough by now."

"Nonsense! Of course I shall," Emmaline replied with a laugh. "Caroline and Adeline will excuse me."

Both gentlemen bowed and she led the way. Jeremy's first thought upon seeing Sir Osbert's bedroom was that it suited the gentleman perfectly. The furniture was of solid oak and built on sturdy lines, giving an impression of heaviness as did the draperies and carpets. Then he saw Sir Osbert propped up in his bed and he wondered if this frail fellow was really his old mentor. A moment later Emmaline stood by his side and Jeremy saw once again the familiar flash of humor in Sir Osbert's eyes.

"Hello, Gilbert. Who is this young puppy you've brought with you, today?" Delwyn demanded of Lord Barnett, determined to make things difficult for the boy.

"Come, come," Gilbert chided his old friend. "Either your memory or your eyesight is failing. You ought to recollect Jeremy."

"So I would have," Osbert retorted, "if it hadn't been so long since I've seen him and if he didn't look like such an absurd dandy!"

In spite of himself Jeremy laughed. "No, no, sir, you are quite out there! A true dandy would be horrified to be compared to a philistine such as myself."

Grudgingly Sir Osbert nodded. His voice was a trifle kinder as he said, "Come here, lad, and let me look at you. It's been too many years since you used to run wild here. Now I understand it's London where you do so."

Something caught at Jeremy's throat as he remembered the days when this gruff neighbor of his father had been the only adult he had felt he could go to with his problems. The memory, long thrust aside, came back with a rush of the same affection that had been so strong between them then. "It's been a long time, sir," he said as he moved to stand beside the bed.

"Aye, too long," Osbert agreed. "You needn't have feared contagion from my illness."

"I did not," Jeremy said grimly.

At this point Gilbert coughed. "Yes, well it was I who kept the boy away," he explained awkwardly. A muscle twitched in Jeremy's cheek and he looked away as his father continued, "I thought, you see, when you were so ill at first, that the last thing you needed was Jeremy badgering you with his nonsense and troubles. I told him he wasn't to call upon you until he could do so with something good to report of himself."

"And that, of course, has not been possible," Jeremy added, once more falling into the mincing tones his father hated.

Sir Osbert closed his eyes a moment. When he opened them again, he said, "I wish you had come, Jeremy. I wouldn't have minded."

There was a flash of something between the two men, one young, one old, then silence fell as all three turned to look at Emmaline. "My dear, please wait downstairs with your sisters," Sir Osbert said quietly. "I shall be quite all right with these two fellows."

With a smile and an uneasy feeling, Emmaline agreed. When she was gone, the two older men turned and looked at Jeremy and waited.

"Well?" Sir Osbert said at last. "Haven't you something to ask me?"

Jeremy looked quizzically at his father, but his voice was mild as he spoke to the man in the bed. "I suppose I have. We may as well speak bluntly, Sir Osbert, for it is clear to me that my father's scheme is well known to you. He wishes me to marry your daughter Emmaline. Is that your wish as well?"

"Dash it all, boy, what is that to the point?" Osbert demanded with a flash of his old strength. "Do you wish to marry her? And will she have you if you do?

Once more Jeremy looked away. "As to whether she will have me, I don't know."

"Haven't made good use of your time downstairs, have you?" his father observed sneeringly.

Jeremy ignored his father. Instead he went on speaking to Sir Osbert. "Do I wish to marry your daughter? How can I say? I had not meant to even think of marriage, just yet."

"And Emmaline is not up to the mark of the beauties you've become accustomed to, is that it?" Sir Osbert observed shrewdly.

Jeremy turned and moved next to the bed again. He took the hand Sir Osbert held out to him, gripping it firmly. "Never mind," Delwyn went on gently. "I know my daughter ain't a beauty. But neither is she precisely an antidote. She's had her share of offers, I'll tell you."

At Lord Barnett's start of surprise he said, a trifle waspishly, "You needn't look so confounded, Gilbert! Just because neither she nor I are ones to boast of her conquests don't mean she hasn't had any. Emmaline turned 'em all down and I can't say as I blame her, though I wish she were settled. Still, she's a good girl and she would make you a good wife, Jeremy. But I'm not a man to force such a match on anyone. And were circumstances otherwise, I would say you ought to wait until you did feel ready to marry. But your father, God help him, is determined that you shall marry, and right soon. Nothing I've said will sway him and, frankly, I'm not altogether certain he's wrong."

"And you would trust your daughter to me?" Jeremy asked in a voice that betrayed none of the turmoil he felt.

"Aye," Delwyn agreed. "If you'll give me your word you'll not hurt her."

Jeremy met Sir Osbert's gaze steadily. "I suppose you've heard all the worst gossip about what I've done these past few years in London. I won't try to tell you it's not true for most of it probably is. But if I marry your daughter, I swear I shall do my best to please her."

"That's all I ask of you, Jeremy," Sir Osbert said.

"Good. That's settled then," Gilbert said briskly. "All you've got to do is go downstairs and ask the girl to marry you."

"All?" Jeremy chided his father.

Lord Barnett regarded his son levelly. "That shouldn't be too difficult for you. You've quite the touch with the ladies, at least those of the demi-monde. Charm her. Flatter her. Whatever need be. Just get her agreement and let's get on with the wedding."

Jeremy bowed and left. If his temper was not entirely subdued, nevertheless he managed it well as he slowly, thoughtfully descended the steps to the first floor.

Upstairs, the chessboard was set up and waiting as Emmaline had predicted. It was not until the men had made their first few moves that Sir Osbert spoke to the matter at hand. "Well, come, come, how did he take the news when you told him what you wanted?" he demanded, unable to control his impatience any longer. "Furious, I'll wager, though he was pleasant enough here."

Gilbert's eyes took in the pallor of his neighbor's face and concern etched itself upon his own. Nevertheless he rallied to say as he moved a pawn, "At first he was enraged and unwilling to believe that I meant what I said. I don't doubt he could have cheerfully strangled me. But for all his faults Jeremy is a realist and so he came around to the notion soon enough. Indeed, I'll wager Jeremy is downstairs right now doing the pretty with your three daughters. He can be quite charming with the ladies when he so chooses. Of that his escapades have left me no doubt."

"Hrrumph," Osbert snorted, retaliating with a knight. "Adeline and Caroline are already provided for. It's Emmaline I'm worried about."

"Yes, well, I agree. I am not altogether pleased that they are here," Gilbert countered. "Caroline and Adeline are attractive young women, married or not, and I am afraid that by contrast Emmaline seems something of a drab wren today. Not that I think so," he added hastily. "You know that I have the greatest regard for the child and think her worth ten of any other young lady I know. But I am afraid my son has been so jaded by the birds of paradise he sees in London that he will fail to value her as I do."

"I have never thought Jeremy a fool," Osbert

replied equably. He paused, then added with less certainty, "But is he shrewd enough to understand that Adeline and Caroline have the luxury of indulging their fancies for new hairdos and clothes and frivolous things, I wonder. The sorts of things I should like for Emmaline. Or if he'll realize that with a little pampering she could well outshine her sisters. Certainly if one is considering kindness and consideration and intelligence, she already does. Will your young son think so?"

Gilbert looked down at the chessboard, chin in hand. "Perhaps. But whether he does or not I have made it clear to the boy that I have the means to compel him to marry. And that I should favor a match with your daughter."

Reluctantly Osbert nodded. "Aye, and I'll admit I've always had an affection for Jeremy myself. But what you tell me about his latest adventures fills me with misgivings. Still, it may answer. I cannot imagine any man resisting Emmaline's good nature."

Gilbert patted his friend's hand, then moved his queen. "Jeremy will not, I'll see to that. If need be, I'll send the boy away and look after Emmaline myself," he concluded grimly.

Sir Osbert looked distressed. "You know," he said, "I cannot bring myself to think Jeremy is really all that bad. He's just fallen in with the wrong company and Emmaline may be just what he needs to bring him round again."

"I think it more likely that he's gone looking for the wrong company," Gilbert countered. "But I hope you may be right."

Osbert moved a bishop. "Mind you, though," he said warningly, "I'll see them both together before

I give my final approval to the match. Ah, but it would be good to see my Emmaline settled before I die. I worry about her, you know. A woman alone is not an enviable creature. Check."

"What? Where?" Gilbert demanded, turning all his attention to chess. Moving his king at last, he said "You haven't beaten me yet, old friend."

3

NEAR the bottom of the stairs, Jeremy paused as he heard voices coming from a room to his right. A moment's reflection was all that was needed to remind him that the persons speaking must be in the old-fashioned parlor he had always loved. He found himself wondering if there had been many changes made to the room since he last had seen it. Then his attention was caught by the words he overheard and cold rage washed over him.

Emmaline and her sisters had come into the parlor while the Barnetts were upstairs and Adeline and Caroline were now all aflutter. "*Such* a dreadful reputation," Adeline said tremulously.

"Yes, but as handsome as ever." Caroline sighed. "Mind you, I love my Frederick dearly but I confess I have always felt a fondness for Jeremy. Do you remember when he danced at our comeout balls here at the house?"

"You were too young for that, Emmaline, but he was the most excellent of dancers," Adeline agreed with a condescending smile. "If not the most polite. He had a way of poking fun at one that was horrid."

"I have always found him kind enough," Emmaline replied tranquilly.

"Oh, pooh!" Caroline scoffed. "You were always at his heels and he was always chasing you away. Always chasing all of us away, for that matter. Sometimes I used to think that the only ones of us he liked were Mama and Papa."

Remembering how a strong arm had steadied her in the rain that fell the day they buried her mother and the curtness with which he had then bid her farewell, Emmaline could not entirely disagree. Nevertheless she said, "Yes, but there were times when he did not chase us away. Once he even took me fishing. He would have taken you as well had you wished to go. And when my favorite doll was broken, he contrived to mend her."

"More than likely he was the one who broke it," Adeline countered, conveniently forgetting that it had actually been she who had done it in a fit of sisterly jealousy.

"I wonder why he came to call upon Papa," Caroline said eagerly. "Do you suppose he has come down from London in disgrace?"

Adeline sniffed. "I haven't a doubt of it. And why he should be bothering Papa I cannot imagine."

This, however, was too much for Emmaline. "Papa wished to see him," she said firmly. "Indeed, I shouldn't be surprised if Papa invited him to come and call."

"Oh, Emmaline, you have always made excuses for the fellow," Adeline said impatiently.

"Yes," Caroline echoed. "Next we shall be expecting to hear the news of your betrothal to Jeremy Barnett!" she added with a malicious titter.

This notion seemed so exquisitely absurd that it sent the two sisters into gales of laughter. At this moment Jeremy entered the parlor and said in his mincing voice, "My, my, the two of you grow more shrill with each passing year. Is that why you take refuge here instead of with your husbands?"

Shooting dagger glances at young Barnett, the two sisters rose. In a frosty voice Adeline said, "My dear Emmaline, we must be going. Hubert is expecting me, and Frederick is expecting Caroline back in time for lunch. We shall call upon you next week as always. Mr. Barnett, good day. How unfortunate that I cannot say it has been a pleasure."

With great irony Jeremy bowed deeply and stepped aside to let the ladies pass. When Emmaline had seen them out to their carriage she returned to the parlor where Jeremy was still waiting for her. In a mild voice she said, "Must you offend them always? After all we are no longer children to forever be at daggers drawn."

Jeremy had been playing with the cord of a well-remembered curtain and now he let it fall as he faced Emmaline. "It has been some time since I was a child," he said curtly. He knew, however, as well as she how badly he had behaved and already he was regretting it. The mincing voice was gone as he added, "Forgive me. My wretched tongue. But I have never been able to abide fools."

"It was not so difficult for you to be civil to them before you went upstairs," Emmaline observed shrewdly.

Jeremy hesitated. "Before I went upstairs I did not yet wish to speak with you alone, and now I do. Besides, the things I heard your sisters say were, well, the outside of enough."

Emmaline moved closer to Barnett. "I was afraid you had," she said. "You ought not to have eavesdropped, of course, but I can offer no excuses for my sisters either. What I do not understand is why you wished to speak with me alone. Is it about my father?" He shook his head and she persisted, "Are you in trouble, then? Is there any way I can help?"

Jeremy smiled down at her sardonically and with one hand gently touched her cheek. "My dear Emmaline," he murmured. "You always were so loyal. And yet, I confess it is not entirely flattering to me that you immediately assume I have landed myself in the briars."

Aware of a rising warmth within herself to match what she saw in his eyes, Emmaline stepped away from Jeremy. A trifle breathlessly she said, "Oh, are you not? I am sorry then. I fear I am taking after my sisters. What is the reason you wished to speak with me?"

As she waited, Emmaline could not help but regret, as she had since his arrival, that the dress she wore was sadly out of date. For the first time in a long while she wished she had taken more pains with her hair. Particularly when she looked at Jeremy, resplendent in his coat of blue Bath cloth, biscuit-colored trousers, polished boots, and neatly tied neckcloth. Already shaken, she was completely undone when he came forward and grasped her hand. There was a kindness in his voice that she remembered all too well as he said, still ignoring her question, "How do you go on, Emmaline? It cannot be easy with your father ill and you the one to always be looking after him."

Coloring, Emmaline looked down, afraid to meet Jeremy's eyes. "You are kind, but I have grown accustomed, some time since, to my situation," she said quietly.

"Well so your father has not," Jeremy replied gently. "He wishes far more for you. A husband, a family perhaps."

Snatching back her hand, Emmaline hastily turned away. "You need not roast me," she said with dignity. "I know very well that I am all but on the shelf. At my last prayers, in fact. But I cannot change what it is."

"No, but I should like to alter your situation," Jeremy said gently from a point just above and behind her shoulder.

Puzzled, Emmaline turned to face him. "What are you trying to say to me?" she demanded warily. "What harebrained scheme have you hatched this time?"

A wry smile upon his face, Jeremy said, "None, my dear Emmaline. What I am trying to say, so wretchedly I fear, is that I should like you to become my wife."

All the colors drained from Emmaline's face and she found herself sitting down in the nearest chair. "What did you say?" she asked at last.

Bitterness twitched at Jeremy's lips as he said, "I have asked you to marry me, Miss Delwyn. Apparently my proposal was a far greater shock to you than I had anticipated; I am sorry. I had not realized how thoroughly news of my reputation must have reached you."

Abruptly he knelt in front of her. "Were there more time, I should have courted you for the weeks or months that custom prescribes. With your father's illness, however, it is his own wish that I should not wait. And I need no such time to know my own heart." He hesitated, then added, "We are not entirely strangers. You know me well enough to know that I do not dance to the tune of convention nor do I think that you do. But if your father should die before we were married, then the wedding would have to be put off some months at the least, perhaps a year, and your father does not wish that to happen."

"You, you have already spoken to my father?" Emmaline said in astonishment. "And he approves?"

Jeremy cocked his head. "Did you think me so lost to all decency that I would speak to you first? Ask him, if you will, what he thinks of the notion. Then give me your answer. I shall wait right here, if you wish, while you do."

A trifle dazed, Emmaline stood and Jeremy stood with her. "Yes, yes," she said absently, "perhaps that would be best. Pray excuse me. I shall return shortly."

Upstairs she found her father and his friends talking quietly. At the sight of her stunned face, Lord Barnett rose to his feet. "Shall I leave the two of you alone?" he asked.

Emmaline put out a hand to stop him. "No. Please. This concerns you as much as my father, I believe. Papa, is it true that you wish me to marry Jeremy Barnett?"

"I wish you to marry whomever you will. You know I have never pressed you to choose against your own inclinations. But I did think you liked the boy," Sir Osbert countered. "Has Jeremy said he wishes to marry you?" Emmaline nodded and he went on, "What did you tell him?"

Her eyes began to dance. "I didn't answer. I was too astonished, I'm afraid, to do so."

"Do you very much dislike the idea?" Gilbert asked, his expression held rigidly impassive.

Emmaline turned to face her father's friend. "No," she said honestly, "I cannot say that I dislike the notion. I have long felt a *tendre* for your son. But I knew that was a foolish fantasy and I did not expect him to feel the same. Indeed, before today I should have said he was all but unaware of my existence save as a sort of annoying younger sister, unrelated though we may be."

Lord Barnett coughed. "Yes, well, young men do not always wear their hearts upon their sleeves. Nevertheless I must say the match has *my* approval. I think it would answer very well, both for you, Emmaline, and for my son Jeremy."

"I should like it as well," Sir Osbert said quietly. "You know I've always had a fondness for the boy and for you. If you married Jeremy, then I should not have to worry what will happen to you when I die. But the decision is yours, Emmaline. I should never wish to press you into anything you would find distasteful."

Emmaline looked at Lord Barnett. "Is he serious in his proposal, your son?"

"Very serious," Barnett answered gravely.

"Why now? Why so suddenly?" she persisted.

"He is aware of my condition, that is part of it, but that doesn't matter," Sir Osbert broke in to say. "I think you will find, my dear, that if you accept Jeremy Barnett, he will do his best to see you happy."

Emmaline hesitated, then bent over to kiss her father's forehead. "Then I shall accept Jeremy's proposal, Papa. And I confess that I feel myself in some sort of wonderful dream. Shall I bring him back upstairs now?"

Sir Osbert's eyes twinkled perceptibly as he replied, "After you have given Jeremy suitable time to reply to your acceptance, my dear. After all, he may wish to express his pleasure, you know."

With a laugh Emmaline left her father's bedroom. She did not at once return downstairs, however. Instead she went to her room and took her time rearranging her hair and changing her dress to one of blue cambric. The scooped neck and flounced hem were the latest fashion and the color flattered her eyes. It had been her one recent extravagance and now she wore it defiantly downstairs. It was not foolish vanity to wish to appear at one's best for the man one was soon to marry. The fact that Emmaline had so little time of late to think of clothes did not mean that she was unaware of the courage that came with knowing one looked one's best.

Emmaline paused, and admitted to herself that she needed courage right now. There was something about Jeremy that frightened her—he no longer seemed the heedless boy she had fallen in love with so many years before. Instead, he had became the man who now claimed her, and that man was all but a stranger.

Nevertheless, there was a lightness to Emmaline's step as she entered the parlor that with the rest of her transformation made Jeremy regard her with frank amazement and approval. Smiling, she said, "Well, my friend, unless you have changed your mind in the past half hour, then I should very much like to accept your proposal of marriage."

For a moment Jeremy did not move. However happy the change in Emmaline's appearance, he nevertheless felt suddenly trapped as a wild beast might when snared in a net. But then he was all courtesy as he possessed himself of Emmaline's hand and smiled in return. "I am delighted," he said.

Emmaline lowered her eyes, conscious of her heart racing at the warmth that seemed to fill Jeremy's eyes. Before she could protest, he took her in his arms and kissed her. At first it was a gentle kiss, meant more as a token gesture than anything else. Then, as though a devil possessed him, he could not help kissing her with a growing insistence that forced her own lips apart as his arms tightened around her and hers around him. Jeremy broke off first, leaving Emmaline breathless.

A trifle frightened by feelings she had not known were in her, Emmaline stammered hastily, "My—my father would like to see you. Us. Right now."

"Of course," he said, stepping back. Silently he cursed himself for frightening her. After all, there was no need. She would be his wife soon enough and then there would be time to discover the truth of her nature, something that must in no way affect his decision to marry Emmaline. Theirs was, after all, an arranged marriage of sorts, and should she prove cold after the wedding, why then Jeremy would scarcely be at a loss to find warmth elsewhere. At that he was already an expert. It was madness to risk everything this way.

With an attempt to make amends he asked her gently, "Have I shocked you? I did not mean to. You were so beautiful just then, and I felt so fortunate. But let us go up and tell our fathers the good news."

Swiftly Emmaline's eyes rose to meet his. "Yes. I think they would like that," she said honestly.

With a half bow, Jeremy offered her his arm.

Seated side by side, Lord Barnett and Sir Osbert received their children with warm congratulations. Lord Barnett went so far as to rub his hands together and say briskly, "Good. Now that's settled, when shall we set the date for? Three weeks? Four? Or shall I arrange for a special license and we hold the wedding as soon as it arrives?"

Emmaline could not but be aware of how Jeremy stiffened beside her, and her own impulse was to protest. But there was no need. Sir Osbert spoke for them. "No, Gilbert," he said firmly. "I'll not have these two rushed into things. The betrothal announcement shall be sent out as quickly as you wish and all the relatives, on both sides, notified. But I'll not have the date set until these two have had more time to come to know one another."

"More time to know one another?" Gilbert demanded, his color and voice rising. "But they grew up on neighboring estates and have known one another all their lives!"

"You forget, Gilbert, that by your decree Jeremy has not been by here for some number of years. Moreover, I'll not have the pair of them bullied into a hurried marriage," Sir Osbert countered. "I've no wish, even if you are indifferent to gossip, to have it bandied about that there was something havey-cavey about the business. You don't wish it said, do you, that this was a matter of urgency?"

Gilbert halted in midprotest as the meaning of

Osbert's words sank in. After a moment he said, "You are right, of course, old friend. Very well. We shall not yet set the date. But I am sure," he added, fixing his son with a firm stare, "that my son will wish to spend as much time as possible getting to know, as you put it, his fiancée."

"By all means," Sir Osbert agreed cordially. "But for now, off with the pair of you. You may call again tomorrow, Jeremy."

Jeremy bowed, said all that was polite, and took his leave with his father. That unhappy gentleman kept a civil tongue, but even Emmaline could guess he would have a great deal to say when he reached home.

4

OVER the next several days, Emmaline had to endure the delight of her father's entire staff over her impending marriage, even as her own uneasiness grew, an uneasiness she had no explanation for. Jeremy came to call every day and he was attentive and amusing, and yet she could not help but feel that something was wrong.

Mrs. Bailey, however, was in raptures as she said, "*Such* a handsome face! And such excellent manners. You must be so happy, Miss Emmaline. And may I say we are all so happy as well to know that you will soon be settled so comfortably."

Emmaline toyed with the tassle of a curtain as she said, "Yes, well thank you, Mrs. Bailey. But there is no question of an immediate wedding, you know. Not so long as Papa—"

"Oh, go on with you," Mrs. Bailey scoffed. "As though your father would allow that to interfere. I happen to know he has already spoken with Dr. Farley, who said that there would be time to send for you should your papa take a turn for the worse while you were on your honeymoon. And Mrs. Colton has offered to come and look in upon your father every day if he wishes. Once you're married."

"Mrs. Colton is a dear lady and has been good to us," Emmaline said with a smile, "but she is scarcely out of mourning for her own husband. How I can I ask her to take on such a task as that?"

Mrs. Bailey sniffed. "You wouldn't have to ask her to take it on. She's already offered."

With a hint of desperation in her voice Emmaline said, "Yes, well, we shan't need that just yet. Neither Mr. Barnett nor I are quite prepared to set the date of our wedding."

"Aye, but that will change in a few days or weeks, you'll see." Mrs. Bailey nodded her head wisely. "Gentlemen *always* become impatient. P'rhaps that's the gentleman's carriage I hear."

To Emmaline's relief—a sensation that did not auger well for the future—it was not Jeremy's curricle the housekeeper had heard but her sister's. "Caroline?" she said with some surprise a few minutes later. "I am delighted to see you, but this is very unexpected."

A trifle breathless, Caroline stepped into the parlor, stripping off her gloves as she did so. She kissed Emmaline upon the cheek and then sat beside her on the sofa. "Oh, Emmy, I had to come and see you. Is it true you are to marry Jeremy Barnett?"

Avoiding her sister's eyes, Emmaline said, "Why, yes, are you not pleased for me?"

"No!" Caroline said vehemently. At Emmaline's startled look she possessed herself of both her sister's hands and said, "I know you have always had a fondness for him, Emmaline, and I know that in spite of everything anyone may say he is still the most eligible *parti* hereabouts and I ought to be very happy for your sake, but I am not. Not unless he has spoken to you of love. Has he?"

"N-no," Emmaline admitted slowly. Then she asked, bewildered, "But how can you disapprove? Wasn't your own betrothal to Frederick much the same? I don't recall that he spoke of love, though we all knew you loved him. Didn't you feel the same astonished happiness when he offered for you?"

It was Caroline's turn to look away. She took a deep breath, then said, "I see I must tell you the whole sordid story."

And so she did. With increasing dismay Emmaline heard a tale of love on her sister's part paired with contempt and increasing desertion by her husband. What had begun as a light affair when Caroline had been pregnant with her first child had become a way of life for Frederick. Indeed, he scarcely bothered to treat her with civility anymore.

"Surely it cannot be as bad as that?" Emmaline protested, appalled when her sister was done.

"It is far worse, I assure you," Caroline countered. "Frederick never wished to marry me; it was his mother's wish. He is forever telling me so. Oh, Emmaline, there are times when I think I cannot bear it. But what choice do I have? Only I could not bear to think you might repeat my mistake and I felt I must warn you. If I am mistaken and your betrothal to Jeremy is not as mine was to Frederick, then I beg you to forgive me. And I pray you will not be angry with me."

"How could I be angry?" Emmaline asked warmly

as she embraced her hapless sister. "I know you have come to try to help me."

"Then you will think about what I have said?" Caroline demanded.

"I will think about what you have said," Emmaline assured her. "But what are we to do about you?"

"Nothing," Caroline said quietly.

"But Papa would never stand for—" Emmaline began.

"Papa's *health* would never stand for him to know the truth," Caroline broke in wearily. "And you needn't think it would do any good for you to speak to Frederick. He only laughs when his own mother tells him he is behaving terribly toward me. No, I am trapped, but you need not be."

When her sister left shortly thereafter, Emmaline went upstairs, determined to beard her father.

Not quite certain of how to begin, she spoke somewhat hesitantly. "Papa, will you tell me what is really afoot? Why Jeremy proposed to me."

Sir Osbert tried to evade her eyes. "What do you mean, child?" he asked querulously. "The boy wishes to marry you, you wish to marry him, what more is there to say?"

"A great deal," she countered. "I believed this—this Banbury tale at first, that he had come to care for me. But somehow I begin to wonder now, and I mean to have the truth. Did circumstances or Lord Barnett compel Jeremy to ask for my hand?"

"Do you think Lord Barnett, or anyone for that matter, could compel that young man to do something he did not wish to do?" Sir Osbert asked with mock amazement.

"Yes," Emmaline retorted bluntly. "I like Lord Barnett but a more ruthless man I have never met. And however determined Jeremy may be, we all know that he is vulnerable to Lord Barnett's commands because he is forever short of funds—if half the gossip that reaches us is to be believed. Indeed, I have no doubt that is precisely the reason Lord Barnett refuses to settle any property on his son."

"Very well." Osbert sighed. "I shall tell you the truth. But I want no missishness from you, do you hear? Gilbert has threatened to cut Jeremy off without a penny, while he is alive, if he does not marry—and soon. Gilbert even suggested you as a suitable bride."

"I see," Emmaline said thoughtfully. "And yet you told me to accept him."

"I told you to do as your heart bid you. This changes nothing," Osbert protested angrily. "Some of the best marriages are arranged. Your mother's and mine was. And Jeremy did agree to it without, I thought, any evidence of distaste."

"So he did," Emmaline conceded with a complaisance that made her father wary. "As did I."

"Please give the notion a chance," Sir Osbert begged her. "I want very much to see you settled before I die, and it's no use telling me I won't die soon. For all the nonsense that fool of a doctor tells me, I know the truth."

For a long moment Emmaline was silent. "Very well," she said at last, hiding her disquiet, "I shall give it a chance."

"Good!" Osbert said emphatically. "That is all I ask. Now have them send up my lunch."

"Of course, Papa," she said as she kissed his brow. Then, very thoughtful, she went to do as he had bid.

* * *

It would be too much to say that Jeremy Barnett was pleased with the situation in which he found himself, but he was determined to make the best of it. To his delight he discovered that Miss Delwyn possessed far more sensible conversation than most of the chits he had met in London. He had forgotten the fine mind that had listened to and grasped all the things he had explained to her when they were both children. True, she leaned toward a self-assurance that led her often to disagree with him, but that was a welcome relief from young ladies who echoed everything he said, and should it become bothersome, surely such contrariness could be altered in time. Moreover, now that she had accepted his proposal, Miss Delwyn expended far more thought and energy upon her appearance. All in all, he thought she would do. If he had to marry.

So Jeremy sent the announcement of his betrothal to the London papers and tried to ignore the panic that threatened, from time to time, to overwhelm him. Scarcely to his surprise, within the week his best friend, Edward Hastings, appeared on his doorstep. He arrived as Jeremy was about to climb into his own curricle to take Emmaline out for a drive. Instead, Jeremy watched the phaeton pulled by two neatly matched grays draw to a halt at the front steps of Barnett Hall. "Edward!" he cried as he went to meet his friend. "How delightful to see you, you old devil!"

Hastings handed the reins over to his diminutive tiger and then raised his quizzing glass in a gesture more foppish than any Jeremy had ever adopted. After regarding his good friend for several seconds and noting the twinkle in Jeremy's eyes, he drawled, "Odd, you don't look as though you have taken leave of your senses."

"I have not," Jeremy replied cheerfully.

"Then what," Hastings demanded, "is the meaning of that absurd notice in the *Gazette*?"

"Ah, that." Jeremy nodded wisely. "I am getting married."

Hastings appeared to stagger. "So I was right: you have taken leave of your senses."

Jeremy laughed. "No, I have not, as I will prove to you shortly. In fact, why don't you come with me and meet Emmaline? Hargraves can take care of your luggage."

"Very well," Hastings said with a deep sigh. "If I must meet this creature, I must."

Jeremy only laughed again and steered his friend to the curricle. "I shan't be needing you after all," he told his groom. "Stand away from their heads."

As the groom stepped back, the chestnuts pulled neatly away down the drive and Jeremy began to explain. "Now mind, Edward, I've no desire for anyone else to know what I'm about to tell you. That wouldn't look good for either Emmaline or me. But you may as well know the truth. M'father called me home, as I told you in London he had, and as we suspected, he had heard about that bit at Covent Gardens. Well, when I arrived, m'father informed me that either I marry—at once—or he intended to cut off my allowance. Not diminish it, mind you, but cut it off entirely and make it difficult for me to go to the penny-a-pound men for a loan."

"You were in a bind," Hastings agreed sympathetically, all trace of affectation gone now. "And

Miss, er, Delwyn is to be the blushing bride? How did they compel her to agree? Has she a squint or something?"

Jeremy laughed uncomfortably. "Nothing of the sort. We have known one another for years, and like her father, she has had an affection for me, I suppose."

"I see. So all is bliss?" Hastings suggested.

"Not precisely," Jeremy said after a moment's hesitation.

"What is it?" Edward asked quietly. "Is she vulgar? Or something of a peagoose with not two thoughts to rub together in her head?"

There was a longer hesitation this time before Jeremy replied. "On the contrary. Emmaline is exceedingly well bred. And intelligent. She can converse on any subject you might choose and has a great deal of common sense."

"Say no more," Hastings said in a tone of mock horror. "She sounds appalling."

Irritably Jeremy replied, "Oh, do give over your nonsense, Edward. She is nothing of the sort. In fact, I wager you will like her quite well. *I* like her quite well."

"Then what is the problem?" Hastings asked.

"I'm not certain I wish to be married at all!" Jeremy blurted out. "In fact, I am quite certain I don't."

"Then why did you propose?" Edward asked reasonably.

"Because I thought she would be a timid mouse of a thing, given that she has meekly spend the last several years nursing her father, and I could set her up at Barnett Hall while I went up to London anytime I wished," Jeremy said in exasperation. "And anyway my father's threats left me little choice. Would *you* care to have tried to name a respectable young lady of our acquaintance I could have chosen instead?"

"No," Hastings agreed dryly.

"Unfortunately, now I find that I don't think it will do. Dash it all, this would have to be a *real* marriage!" Jeremy replied gloomily. "And I doubt very much I am ready for that."

"Do you mean to back out?" Hastings asked carefully. "It is all the fashion, what with Lady Charlotte renouncing the Prince of Orange."

"Yes, and look at her father's reaction to that! Threatening to make her a virtual prisoner if what I hear is to be believed," Jeremy countered. "No," he said decisively. "I cannot forget that m'father's threat still hangs over my head. Besides, I am not such a blackguard as to serve Miss Delwyn a turn like that."

"My dear boy," Hastings said, resuming his affectation, "I feel for you!"

5

JEREMY and Edward soon arrived at Sir Osbert's home. As they climbed down from the curricle Hastings looked about him approvingly and said, "So the girl does not come penniless by the looks of this place. Has she any sisters?"

"Both married," Jeremy said witheringly, "and sharp-tongued into the bargain."

"Just as well," Hastings said philosophically. "Someone must maintain the torch of bachelorhood, but rest assured I shall lend you support at your wedding."

"How kind of you," Jeremy retorted with spirit. "But have a care or I'll take my revenge by finding you a wife as well. Aye, and betroth you to her before you or she knows what you are about."

"Just knock at the door," Edward said derisively.

Jeremy did so and they were admitted by Bailey. He, however, was unaware that Emmaline had taken refuge with her thoughts in the garden and it took Jeremy some while to find her. Indeed, his temper was more than a little frayed by the time he and Hastings tracked her down by the roses.

Emmaline had tried desperately to stifle her

unease, but when she saw Jeremy arrive with a stranger, she knew it was no use. They paused, then came forward and Emmaline watched Jeremy grow paler as he approached her. She could not deceive herself that his expression held any happiness and Caroline's words echoed in her ears.

"Hallo, Emmaline," Jeremy said with a determined smile. "May I present Edward Hastings, a good friend—in fact my dearest friend. Edward, this is my fiancée, Miss Delwyn."

Hastings bowed promptly. "Delighted, ma'am. Best wishes and all that."

"Thank you," Emmaline said with a smile she did not feel. "Are you just come from London?"

Hastings nodded. "Read the news and had to come see what it was all about."

"Jeremy's betrothal being such a strange event?" Emmaline suggested cordially.

"Exactly, I—" Hastings broke off in confusion as he realized where his tongue was headed.

"It's all right, Edward," Jeremy said with a sharp laugh, "Miss Delwyn is noted for her quick wits."

"Here! I say, Jeremy," Hastings remonstrated.

It was Emmaline's turn to laugh. "It's all right, Mr. Hastings," she said with a kindness she did not feel. After a pause, she added, "Jeremy, I do wish, however, that we might speak privately, for a few minutes."

Jeremy's eyebrows rose in surprise but after a moment he bowed and said, "Of course. Shall we go into the parlor? Edward can continue to admire your garden."

"Wonderful garden," Hastings agreed promptly. "Delighted to wait here for you."

"Thank you," she told him warmly, then led the way inside.

Once there, however, Emmaline set down the flower basket she was holding but could not seem to bring herself to speak. In the end it was Jeremy who broke the silence. "What is it, my dear?" he asked gently. "You seemed quite distressed just now, outside."

Almost undone by his kindness, Emmaline turned away, forcing herself to be resolute. Coolly she said, "You are an excellent actor, are you not, Jeremy? Did I not know better I should indeed think you were my devoted fiancé. But my father has admitted to me the circumstances of—of our betrothal. How devastated you must have been to be forced into something so distasteful to you."

Behind her Emmaline heard a sharp intake of breath. The coolness in his voice matched her own as Jeremy replied, "How unfortunate that he told you. May I ask what it is that you wish to tell me?"

Emmaline turned to face him. In a softer voice she said, "Let us speak frankly, Jeremy, shall we? You are no more happy in our betrothal than I am, are you?"

"What do you mean?" he asked warily.

Emmaline looked at her hands. She was careful to keep her voice steady as she said, "I see very well how you flinch each time anyone asks about the wedding. And as I said, my father has told me everything. I cannot help but feel our betrothal was a mistake." Jeremy's face darkened and she hastened to add, "I have known you almost all of my life and yet we are all but strangers to one another. You don't wish to marry me, nor am I at all certain I wish to marry you. That does not bode well for the future, I fear."

Jeremy stood quite still, conscious of a sense of shock. He had joked with Edward over the difficulties of finding a woman to marry him. The truth was, however, that he had never doubted that his title, wealth, and lineage would make him acceptable to any woman his choice should settle on. "I had thought you cared for me," he said at last.

He could not guess what it cost Emmaline to shrug and say lightly, "Ah, well, it seems I had mistaken my heart, as these last few days have so clearly shown me."

"Yes, well, what is that to say to the matter?" Jeremy asked roughly, turning away. "You say that your father told you my circumstances. We are betrothed and the reasons for that betrothal have not changed on my part. And there is still your father's concern for you."

"So there is," Emmaline agreed, looking at his back steadily. "That is what I wish to talk with you about. I know you are right, but Jeremy, surely you see that a marriage between us won't work? What are we to do? If we break the betrothal your father will cut you off without a penny and mine—" Emmaline's voice broke and it was a moment before she could go on. "Dr. Farley has told me he believes my father has no more than six months to live, and I cannot bear to risk that he might take a turn for the worse. Or that he should spend his last months in fear for me."

"Yes, well, at any rate we are fortunate in that your father insisted there be no immediate wedding," Jeremy retorted. "Perhaps in time you will find I am not such an intolerable fellow, after all."

"Long or short betrothal, it is a mistake," Emmaline persisted gently.

There was a long silence. "What do you wish to do?" Jeremy asked stiffly.

"Well, I had thought we might pretend we were still betrothed, but not be," she answered forthrightly. "Just until my father . . . until my father dies, or you find someone else to marry. You and I would know the truth, of course, but no one else," Emmaline concluded quietly.

"A masquerade?" he managed to ask at last.

"Yes," Emmaline agreed. "I know it sounds absurd but I can see no other answer. My only fear is that I shall prove a poor liar and my father will read the truth in my face."

For some time Barnett was silent, his eyes fixed on the view from the parlor window. At last he said, "He could not if you were not here. We could go to London. From there you could send back glowing reports of our betrothal."

"I cannot leave my father," Emmaline said with quiet dignity. "Not when he is so ill."

Jeremy could not help but be aware of the determination in her voice, and after a moment he said, "Give me some time to think about the matter, my dear. I promise I shall find us a solution. For the moment, however, let me go back out to the garden and find my friend before he thinks himself deserted."

"Of course," she said at once. "I am needed in the kitchen anyway."

When she was out of sight, Jeremy found Hastings and began to talk urgently to his friend, putting forth a plan. Edward, with his usual amiability, readily agreed. A short time later, Jeremy was shown in to see Sir Osbert.

"Good day, sir," Jeremy said with genuine affection.

The older man regarded him quizzically from beneath half-closed eyelids. "Hmmph. And what have you come to tell me about today? Trouble with your father again? Second thoughts about your betrothal to my Emmaline?"

Jeremy shook his head. "No trouble, sir. Just a question. Do you think Emmaline has had sufficient time to look about her before she marries?"

"What do you mean?" Sir Osbert asked testily.

Taking a seat next to the older man's bed, Jeremy said earnestly, "It seems to me that Emmaline has led far too sheltered a life here. And forgive me, but after your death she is likely to mourn for some time. I just thought that perhaps she ought to have a taste of London, now, before we are married. I should much dislike to have her feel, in later years, that had she seen London she might have made a different choice. When she marries me, I should like her to feel sure that that is what she wishes to do."

For some time Sir Osbert was silent. Jeremy could not know it but his words had struck a resonant chord in the older man. He had had a good marriage, but those were indeed the words Catherine Delwyn had thrown up at her husband on the rare occasions they had been so uncivilized as to fight. In the end Sir Osbert placed a hand over Jeremy's and said, "You are right, my boy, whatever your own motives in saying all this."

Jeremy had the grace to blush before he went

on, "I've a friend, Edward Hastings, whose mother would be only too happy to have Emmaline come and stay with her. If you like, you could have such an invitation in hand by next week."

"You appear to have given this matter a great deal of thought," Sir Osbert said. "Has Emmaline agreed?"

Jeremy looked down at his hands. "I have only broached the matter in the briefest of terms, sir. You must know she has refused to leave your side. After all these years of nursing you she cannot bear to go."

Sir Osbert nodded. "Aye, especially since that fool of a doctor told her what he won't tell me—that I've not got long to live." He paused and cocked an eyebrow at Jeremy. "Some would say that she and I ought to spend that time together."

Jeremy took a deep breath and met Sir Osbert's eyes squarely. This time he spoke with perfect truth when he said, "Is that what you want, sir? Suppose the doctor is wrong? Suppose you have not six months but a year or two years? Emmaline has already given you the past three. How much more of her life is she to waste shut away in this house? I know you love her, sir. And that she loves you. And that if you die while she is in London, she will grieve all the more. But at least she will have seen London and had the chance to dance and go to the theater and ride in the park. Would you deny her that? Hasn't she a right to some life of her own?" He paused, then added, "She will not go unless you ask her to. Will you, Sir Osbert?"

Slowly Delwyn nodded. "You are right, again, Jeremy. Emmaline is my daughter, not my wife.

Sometimes I've forgotten, these past three years, that I ought to be seeing to her needs and not always the other way round. Very well. You get me that invitation, Jeremy, and I'll see to it that Emmaline goes to London. But you're to go as well, mind, and see that no harm comes to her. I'll hold you to account on that!"

"As you should, sir," Jeremy said quietly, with a smile. "As you should." Reluctantly he rose to his feet, "And now I must go and tell my father our plans. I fear he will not take the news as kindly as you have."

Sir Osbert caught Jeremy's hand one more time. "He's a good man, your father. Just caught up in his own pain all these years." Bitterness touched Jeremy's lips but in the end he nodded and Delwyn added with a twinkle in his eyes, "If he objects, refer him to me. I'll let the old scoundrel trounce me at chess and then I'll talk him round. You'll have your visit to London, you and Emmaline, I promise it."

6

LORD Barnett did indeed storm and rant and rave at his son, but in the end, he gave his assent to the trip to London. He could not deny his old friend, Sir Osbert, this request. Still, he took care to warn Jeremy, "If so much as one breath of scandal reaches me here, I shall be in London the next day to soundly thrash you!"

"Don't worry, sir. I shall look after him," Hastings offered generously.

"Indeed?" Barnett said, favoring his son's friend with a jaundiced eye. "I'm not sure you aren't even worse than he is. But what's done is done. I only hope we do not all live to regret this."

Meanwhile Emmaline had her own reservations. But Mrs. Anna Colton, who had been enlisted to help Sir Osbert persuade her to go, was as stubborn as Emmaline. She was even there on the morning Emmaline was to leave for London to prevent any last-minute change of plans.

"Now don't worry about a thing, my dear," she told Emmaline with a smile that belied the sternness of her voice. "I shall call upon your father every day to see that he is all right and I promise to send for you at once should he take a turn for the worse."

Emmaline, who had just been upstairs to bid her father good-bye, held her handkerchief tighter. With a forced smile she replied, "I know that you will take excellent care of him, Mrs. Colton. You have always been such a dear friend to all of us, and I know Papa will like having you about. Indeed, he told me so just now. It is just that I cannot shake the thought that it is my duty to be at Papa's side."

"Nonsense," Mrs. Colton said stoutly. "This trip to London is what Sir Osbert wishes for you, and you know Dr. Farley said we are not to upset your papa. And he would be upset if you refused to go."

Impulsively Emmaline hugged Mrs. Colton and turned to her maid, who was trying to gain her attention. "What is it, Mary?" she asked.

The maid curtsied. "The carriage, miss. It's ready and the gentlemen are just now arrived."

"Already? Very well. I shall be out in a moment."

Emmaline could not refrain from running lightly upstairs to say good-bye to her father one last time. He was waiting for her, propped up with pillows and with a far happier look in his eyes than she had seen for some time. "Papa—" she began.

He cut her short, saying as he held out a hand to her, "Hush, child. Go to London and have fun. That is what I wish for you. And you are not to worry about me, do you hear? I shall have Mrs. Colton to order about and bully unmercifully just as I used to do with you, so you need have no fears on my account!"

In spite of herself Emmaline laughed and retorted amiably, "No, indeed. It is Mrs. Colton I see I must fear for." She paused to hug him then, and when she spoke again it was with a voice that was more than a little unsteady. "Oh, Papa, I shall miss you!"

"As I shall miss you," Sir Osbert replied gruffly. "But I have wanted for some time to see you go off and enjoy yourself, and I tell you I shall do better for knowing you are doing so. Who knows, you may even return to find me in better health than ever."

"I wish it might be so," Emmaline said earnestly.

Then, afraid their resolution would fail them, her father added, "Go on now. I heard a carriage drive round some time ago and your escorts will be growing impatient. Tell Jeremy I said he is to take good care of you!"

"I shall. Good-bye, Papa."

A short time later it was a procession of carriages that pulled away from the home Emmaline had always known. She rode in a comfortable chaise-and-four with her maid while Hastings drove his phaeton and Jeremy his curricle. Emmaline didn't quite know whether to take offense at the neglect or give in to her relief at the privacy. In the end, her good nature asserted itself and she gave herself over to the pleasure of watching the countryside.

Mary, however, had other notions. She wished to talk about how handsome Emmaline's betrothed was or how neatly he handled his curricle. As she did so, Emmaline's own treacherous thoughts kept drifting back to how he had kissed her when she accepted his proposal and how her own hands had betrayed her, stealing around his neck. Nor could she forget how her skin seemed to burn whenever he took her hand and how her heart raced until her breath seemed to come in small gasps. No, better not to think of him at all or she might so far forget herself as to go back on her refusal to the marriage. And that way lay madness.

But when they stopped for a neat little luncheon at a posting house along the way, Emmaline's heart once again betrayed her as Jeremy handed her out of the carriage. She could only hope that he did not notice, that his eyes were instead fixed with admiration upon her new dress and bonnet made of rose silk that he had once told her was his favorite color. And she could only be grateful that she did not find herself entirely alone with him but that Hastings was there as well.

Jeremy, with his usual thoroughness, had arranged a private parlor and the dishes were ready within minutes of their arrival. Edward held the chair for her as they sat down. "Comfortable journey so far, Miss Delwyn?" Hastings asked solicitously.

Emmaline smiled at him warmly. "Oh, yes, Mr. Hastings. You and Jeremy appear to have thought of everything. And I still find it difficult to believe your mother has been so kind as to invite me to come and stay with her."

Hastings smiled in return. "M'mother loves company. And going out and about. The happiest I've ever seen her was when she was bringing out m'sister. And m'cousins. Three of 'em in turn."

"Mrs. Hastings must have the warmest heart in London," Jeremy agreed. "I think you'll be happy staying with her. And you need have no fear. She is wonderfully discreet, so that even if she guesses the truth of our betrothal she will tell no one." At Emmaline's look of distress, he added, "Don't mind Hastings, here, he is my oldest friend and entirely discreet as well. I have told him everything."

Emmaline hesitated, then nodded decisively. "All right. I must trust your judgment as to that. But I confess myself still troubled. To what purpose, Jeremy, have you arranged for us to go to London? For I know this must be your doing."

"It will be far easier to convince our fathers we are happily betrothed from London than when we are right under their noses," he answered promptly.

"To be sure," Hastings agreed, pouring her a glass of wine. "A few letters, now and again, detailing your contentment ought to do the trick nicely."

"Yes, but for how long?" Emmaline persisted. "Sooner or later they will press for a wedding, and what then?"

"By then I, we, shall have put a number of plans into action," Jeremy replied curtly. "My first step shall be to consult with my solicitor to see if my father can indeed force his conditions upon me."

"And if he can?" Emmaline asked hesitantly. "However irregular his behavior has been in not yet settling any property or income upon you, that may well be his legal right."

Jeremy's face was grim. "I am all too well aware of that," he told her. "Nevertheless I shall ask. Secondly, I shall lead a model existence for the next few months and perhaps by the time we must break the truth to my father, he will consider me reformed and withdraw his conditions."

"And if that fails?" Emmaline persisted.

For the next few moments Jeremy paid a great deal of attention to his food. In the end, however, he said with a hesitancy that did not suit him, "While we are in London I shall take you about, introduce you to everyone, and generally show you how to behave. Then, after a while, if you cannot attract a desirable *parti* I shall . . . shall eat my hat. Thus your future may be assured."

"How generous. And your own?" Emmaline dryly.

"I had thought you might look about for someone suitable for me. Someone both I and my father will like in the event that I must marry after all."

"It may be a trifle difficult for Jeremy to go about courting anyone else while he is formally betrothed to you," Hastings added helpfully. "Particularly as broken engagements are not much in favor just now, with Lady Charlotte's behavior as an example."

"I see," Emmaline repeated thoughtfully. "So when we break our engagement I may soothe my father with another suitor already to hand and you may satisfy your father with another bride he will approve of. How simple."

Jeremy did not miss the irony in her voice and he answered a trifle sharply, "Nothing of the sort, and I know it as well as you do. It will be the damnedest nuisance for both of us—being hampered about by this formal betrothal. But I, for one, have no other ideas unless you've once more changed your mind about marrying me?"

"Have you changed yours?" she countered.

Glaring eyes met, and in the end it was Hastings

who broke off the duel by saying, "For the moment, I wish the pair of you would simply resign yourself to having a bit of fun before you look for anything else. Jeremy will need time to consult his solicitor, and in any event neither of your fathers is likely to suddenly appear in London to demand a wedding. At any rate, not without warning." He paused, then added thoughtfully, "It would look strange, you know, if there were an open breach right away. Wouldn't want any scandal to get back to 'em."

"Good God, no!" Jeremy agreed with feeling.

"I would not have phrased it precisely that way," Emmaline said calmly, "but my sentiments are the same." Then she added demurely, "And no doubt it will take you some time to properly school me in whom to set my cap for, Jeremy, and what dressmaker to patronize."

"M'mother will take you to the dressmakers," Edward said hastily. "Wouldn't do for Jeremy to be seen taking you to such places. Not the thing at all. Besides, m'mother loves that sort of nonsense. Very hurt if you don't let her do it."

"No, my part will simply be snaring potential husbands to present to you for your approval. As well as seeing that you acquire some town polish," Jeremy added kindly.

"Rubbish!" Emmaline said firmly. "However, I admit I shall be kept quite busy trying to perform the impossible task of finding a female who will meet with both your approval and your father's. I am not even certain it is possible. Particularly as you have no doubt already met all of the eligible young ladies. This is not precisely the beginning of the Season, I know."

"I only ask you to try," Jeremy told her frankly.

With a warm smile Emmaline replied, "And so I shall. This will not be easy for either of us but together we may contrive something that will answer."

"Good," Hastings said approvingly, his hands coming down flat upon the table with a loud sound. "I'm delighted that's settled."

Jeremy eyed his friend for a moment, then said mockingly, "So am I. Now I advise you to attend to your luncheon instead of our affairs so that we may be on our way. I should like to arrive in London before nightfall."

"I am already prepared to leave," Hastings said at once, rising. "Miss Delwyn is not, however, so I think I shall have a walk outside while I wait. No doubt the two of you have things you will wish to talk about anyway without me about. Miss Delwyn, you will excuse me?"

"Yes, do go," Jeremy agreed cordially. "I assure you I shall not mind."

Emmaline glared at her fiancé but politeness made her echo his words. "Pray do as you wish," she said with a forced smile. "No doubt the fresh air will be welcome to you."

As soon as he was gone, Jeremy once more sat facing her across the table and the last of Emmaline's appetite vanished. "Did you—did you wish to say something to me?" she asked him apprehensively.

"That depends. Will you speak frankly with me?" Jeremy answered. "I warn you that I believe it is the only way we may come about."

"Then of course I shall speak frankly," Emmaline replied equably.

"Good. Will you tell me why you have never married," he asked coolly, ignoring her gasp of shock. "Your father told me you have had offers." Emmaline colored angrily and would have protested had his next words not forestalled her. With a kindness she did not expect he said, "I do not mean to distress you, but I cannot help you find another fiancé if I do not know why you are still unwed now. Come, don't be afraid to tell me the truth."

That brought Emmaline's head up with a snap. "I am not afraid," she retorted frostily. "Very well, since you will have it, I turned down all my previous suitors because they were all dead bores. I could not see myself wed to men old enough to be my father or with no more conversation to them than news of the latest hunt."

Jeremy regarded her for a long moment with raised eyebrows, cool amusement evident upon his face. When he answered, his voice matched his face. "Ah, now I comprehend the reason you accepted my proposal! You thought I could scarcely be accused of offering boredom. Upon closer acquaintance, however, you no doubt realized there wasn't anything the least bit interesting about me and that is why you chose to break off our betrothal. But, of course, you were too much the lady to wound me by saying so."

With another flush Emmaline rose from the table and turned her back upon him. "Don't be absurd," she said angrily.

His voice came from behind her and his hands gripped her shoulders as he asked quietly, "No? Then why did you break our betrothal? I know you too well to entirely believe the reasons you have given me."

She did not at once answer and a gentle finger treacherously began to stroke at the back of her neck. Emmaline shivered and after a moment Jeremy turned her around to face him, his strong hands brooking no argument. As her face tilted up at his, an unspoken plea strong in her eyes, something stirred within him. Almost against his will his face came closer and his lips closed upon hers. He meant to be gentle, he meant to kiss her lightly, but the kiss became something more, searing through both of them. Had his arms not slid around her waist, Emmaline's knees would have given way and she would have fallen. Her hands stole up around his neck and she could not help but respond to his demanding lips.

It was Jeremy who abruptly pulled away and turned his back on Emmaline. For what seemed an eternity there was only the sound of their breath coming in broken gasps. Eventually he said, his voice mocking her cruelly, "So, my dear, I had mistaken you. You are not quite the frightened virgin I thought. If it is not fear of what awaits you in our marriage bed that has caused you to break our betrothal, then will you do me the courtesy to tell me what has?"

Emmaline also turned away, not trusting herself to look at him. Her training cried out at how she had forgotten all propriety. With an effort Jeremy could not have guessed at, she forced herself to laugh. She would *not* let him see how much he meant to her. "I *have* told you, sir. I realized that I had mistaken my mind. Once I was naive enough to believe I felt a *tendre* for you and now I have outgrown it."

"Indeed?" His voice still mocked her. "And do you then make a habit of kissing men that way? I warn you it is a dangerous habit."

Unable to stop herself, Emmaline whirled to face him and cried out, "And do you, sir, make a habit of—of forcing your attentions upon well-bred, defenseless young women in inns?"

A cold, harsh look came over Jeremy's face and he bowed. "Forgive me, Miss Delwyn. I had not guessed my attentions were so distasteful to you. I shall take myself away from you at once, and you may follow as soon as you are ready. A word of advice, however. If you do not wish gentlemen to kiss you as I did, then you ought not to agree to be alone with them." As Emmaline gasped in outrage he added contemptuously, "Nor should you put your arms about their necks and respond in kind. A slap across the face is generally considered a far more effective deterrent."

And then he was gone, the door to the parlor closing behind him with a distinct bang. Hastily Emmaline tried to control her agitation before anyone came to look for her. She had scarcely succeeded in doing so when Mary rapped at the door and then, poking in her head, said timidly, "The gentlemen said to tell you the carriages are ready and the hour is growing late."

"Thank you," Emmaline said with a calm she did not feel. "I shall be right there."

7

MRS. Hastings was generally held to be an amiable woman except when it came to her children; she could be truly formidable when aroused and she allowed no interference in their affairs save her own. Indeed, one of the joys of launching her daughter and nieces into the *ton* had been the opportunity to mold their characters to her satisfaction, though always with a certain kindness, of course.

Mrs. Hastings was well liked, however, for her many kindnesses to shy hostesses or anyone who turned to her for advice. While long accustomed to moving in the first circles, she was never so high in the instep as to be above enjoying her company. And although she certainly expected people to listen politely to what she said, she did not demand that they always agree with her notions.

When Edward Hastings asked his mother that she invite Miss Delwyn to London to stay with them, Mrs. Hastings had genially agreed. No doubt the child would require some direction before she was up to the mark. More important than this, however, was the knowledge of her son's interest in the woman. Mrs. Hastings had no desire to be presented with a future daughter-in-law she had not herself approved, and while Miss Delwyn was supposed to be betrothed to Jeremy Barnett, that was information she found difficult to believe.

None of this showed on Mrs. Hastings' face, however, as she received the three young people when they arrived at her London town house, tired and a bit wet from the late afternoon rain that had caught up with them a few miles earlier. Her saloon was decorated in the latest fashion. Green and gold wallpaper was paired with Egyptian furniture, which had legs in the shape of exotic animals. The afternoon being still dark from the recent storm, the candles had already been set out, and their flickering shadows gave the room an even more fantastic look. Mrs. Hastings noted with satisfaction that Emmaline stared about her with patent awe.

Nothing could have exceeded the kindness or good nature Mrs. Hastings showed as she said, "Edward, how good to have you home again. Barnett, I do not stand upon ceremony with you. Congratulations. This is, I collect, Miss Emmaline Delwyn. How do you do, my dear? How was your journey?" Then, without waiting for an answer, she went on, "I am delighted to have you. But please, everyone, sit down. No, no, closer to the fire, Jeremy, to dry out a bit. And you as well, Edward."

Emmaline murmured a greeting, too overwhelmed to know quite what to say. Hastings was more frank. "You've redone the rooms again, Mama. And in such an inconspicuous way!" he said with blatant irony. "And in scarcely a week. You must have had the workmen at it day and night."

"So I did," she agreed with a complacent laugh. "I meant it to be a surprise. Not only for you but for one of my bosom bows who returns to London the day after tomorrow. Do you like it? Or do you find it absurd as Arthur does?"

"Both!" he answered with a laugh of his own. "And I am delighted to see you in such excellent looks, as always, Mama. That is a new gown, I collect?"

Mrs. Hastings happily smoothed the green satin of her skirt as she answered her son. "Well, Edward, the room is quite *comme il faut*, and I thought I ought to be as well. That meant I had to have a few new gowns to match. You will surely admit the need of that?"

"I'll admit nothing of the sort," he retorted good-naturedly. "You just like to buy clothes."

"But I shall admit the need of it, if you like," Jeremy interjected gallantly. "Though I fancy Edward meant that you would always be *comme il faut* no matter what you wore." He paused then added, "I presume that the gown came from Mademoiselle Suzette."

Mrs. Hastings cast a shrewd eye upon her guest. "Want me to take Miss Delwyn there, do you? I'd already planned on doing so. She has superb taste, works quickly, possesses exquisite discretion, and knows how to conceal the gravest flaws in one's figure. Not that that will be a concern with Miss Delwyn," she added, running an expert eye over the girl. "I'd advise a lighter color than the dark blue of her pelisse, however, though the rose gown she is wearing will do well enough. For mornings at home alone, at any rate. My dear, who has had a hand in dressing you?"

"No one save myself," Emmaline answered frankly. "My mother died some years ago and there has been no one else to do so. And, indeed, even I have been hard-pressed to spare the time to look to the matter properly."

"Well, I mean to take you in hand," Mrs. Hastings said kindly. "And soon we shall have you turned out in the latest style."

"Good," Jeremy said frankly. "I shall want my, er, fiancée to have the best of everything. You need not worry, Sir Osbert and not I will be responsible for the bills, which means they will be paid."

Mrs. Hastings raised an eyebrow but made no protest. Instead she turned to Emmaline and said kindly, "No doubt we ought to ask what you would wish, Miss Delwyn. Both Jeremy and I are inclined to ride roughshod over anyone who does not protest. Do you mind?"

With a self-possession she did not entirely feel, Emmaline replied, "How could I? I am very grateful to be able to place myself in your hands, Mrs. Hastings. This is my first visit to London and I cannot pretend that I have the knowledge to choose a *modiste* for myself."

"Very neatly said." Mrs. Hastings nodded approvingly. "Modest, a beauty, and an heiress. Even if you are already betrothed, I think you shall do very well, indeed. But enough of that. How is your father?"

"As well as can be expected," Emmaline replied. "Do you know him?"

"I did," Mrs. Hastings said with a smile. "That was when we were all in our salad days, of course. Not that he spent long in London before he married your mother and bore her off to a house in the country. Catherine Kendrick was her name, as I recall. But while he was here, Lord what a fuss Delwyn kicked up! Ripe for any mischief and such a superb dancer."

While Emmaline tried to reconcile this image of her father with the man she knew, Mrs. Hastings had turned her attention back to Jeremy. "You will be coming to call tomorrow, I presume? And you will be escorting us to any events we attend?"

To Emmaline's surprise he laughed. "From your expression, my dear Mrs. Hastings, I collect you presume nothing of the sort. Instead you mean to recall me to my duty. But you need not, you know. I mean to be a model fiancé and escort my betrothed everywhere I am expected to. Does that reassure you?"

"It might," she retorted amiably, "if I did not know you so well, Mr. Barnett. The more tame you appear, the more suspicious I become. But there, I don't mean to chide you. Will you stay to dinner?"

Lazily Jeremy rose to his feet. "Alas, I regret that I cannot. Edward and I are pledged elsewhere and I must take my leave of you, but I shall come round in the morning."

Mrs. Hastings shook her head decisively. "No, come in the afternoon, Jeremy. I mean to take Miss Delwyn to Mademoiselle Suzette's directly we've finished breakfast tomorrow. She'll know what will suit the girl, and I promise to rely upon her judgment. And you, Edward? I suppose it's no use asking if you'll be home before dawn. I vow we see less of you now than when you were off at school."

With a laugh her son dutifully kissed her cheek and took his farewell with Jeremy. As soon as they were safely gone, Mrs. Hastings moved to the seat next to Emmaline and, clasping her hands together in her lap, said kindly, "Now my dear, you must tell me everything so that I shall know how best to help you. Should you like to make an appearance at Court? Dance at Almack's? Go to an endless round of parties and routs and breakfasts? Or do you wish for a quiet visit and a chance to purchase those things you will need as a bride?"

"I should like to go to parties and dance and shop," Emmaline admitted wistfully. "For I have had very little chance to do any of those things until now. But I do not wish to be a trouble to you."

"Modesty is an excellent trait," Mrs. Hastings said dryly, "but with me you may be as selfish as you choose, and as frank, for I tell you I shall enjoy nothing more than to take you out and about everywhere and listen to any confidences you may wish to share. I assure you I shall enjoy it all! Yes, we must give you a taste of all that London and the *ton* has to offer. But now, you must tell me how you did it. You must tell me how you have managed to snare the *ton*'s most elusive young man and its most cynical one. Are you a sorceress?"

Emmaline laughed. "Would that I were!" she replied. "No, you must give credit where it is due. This was a betrothal arranged by our parents."

Mrs. Hastings' eyebrows rose in astonishment. "Arranged by your parents? Good God, I had not thought Jeremy could be commanded by anyone. It is a pity, however. I had hoped that Jeremy's heart had at last been won. Still, a good many mothers will breathe easier knowing he cannot break their daughters' hearts."

"Has he really such a horrid reputation?" Emmaline asked shyly. "I hoped the reports we had back home were exaggerated."

"Not a bit of it!" Mrs. Hastings answered tartly. "My dear, I do not believe that anyone should enter marriage blindly, and I think it very wrong of your father to allow you such missish dreams about Jeremy. Particularly as even at Selborne you must have heard of his escapades."

Mrs. Hastings paused and her expression softened as she went on, "My dear Miss Delwyn, I do not wish you to think Jeremy a bad bargain. Yes, I wish you to know his reputation, but I also wish you to know that I have often thought Jeremy driven by a devil that love would banish. I have known him to be generous and kind and thoughtful. More so than most young men his age. But never when there is anyone else about to see, if he can help it. It is almost as though he cherishes his reputation as an incorrigible fellow."

"I see," Emmaline said quietly. "No doubt you will find it strange, but I know very little of my fiancé even though Jeremy and I have known one another since I was a small child. These past few years, you see, my father has been ill and his father forbade him to visit us so long ... so long as he could not give a good account of himself. And now our betrothal seems very sudden to me."

Mrs. Hastings nodded wisely. "That's often the way of it." She paused and said shrewdly, "Having regrets, my dear?"

Emmaline straightened her shoulders even though she was unable to meet her hostess's eyes.

"You would be a fool not to," Mrs. Hastings said bluntly. "Not one member of the *ton* would blame you if you broke off this betrothal, though I grant you the gossip would be some time in dying away." Still Emmaline did not reply. As though she understood perfectly, Mrs. Hastings patted Emmaline's hands. "Never mind. Time will tell. Who knows, you may be the one to tame the boy. Now come and tell me about your father. How is his health?"

It required all of Emmaline's strength to be able to reply quietly, "The doctor tells me it is a matter of months before my father dies. Perhaps you will think I should be at his side; that is my own opinion. But he begged me to come to London, and as the doctor said any upset might be fatal I could not argue. There is a neighbor, Mrs. Colton, who has known our family for years. She will look in upon my father every day and both she and the doctor have promised to send word at once should he take a turn for the worse."

"Sensibly said, my dear," Mrs. Hastings told Emmaline approvingly. "No doubt the knowledge his daughter is happily betrothed and enjoying herself in London will serve as a tonic to your father." She paused, then added shrewdly, "And should you have second thoughts, well, you are too far away for your father to read them on your face. He will die happy. But enough of that. It is plain to me that I am distressing you. Come upstairs and see the charming room I have had prepared for you! It was used to belong to my daughter but she is married and now I keep it for my most charming young guests. My dear, I am so looking forward to spoiling you!"

*   *   *

Had he been able to overhear Mrs. Hastings, Jeremy Barnett would not have been displeased. If that lady chose to favor Emmaline with her approval, she would have the *entrée* everywhere—for there were few people who would have the courage not to invite Mrs. Hastings and her protégé to their parties. She was lively and amusing, and if her tongue was occasionally a trifle sharp, one credited that to judgment and not malice. Moreover, not the harshest critic could have faulted the attractiveness of the lady. And as her husband, Mr. Hastings, was also a general favorite, invitations of all sorts always crowded the mantelpiece in their home. Mr. Hastings greatly preferred his clubs and other male pursuits to *ton* parties, but no one held it against Mrs. Hastings that she often attended alone or in the company of friends, both male and female. In another woman this might have given rise to gossip, but Mrs. Hastings was far too upright for that. She was, one might have said, the perfect choice to launch a young lady upon her social career.

Jeremy said something of the sort as they made their way to White's later that evening.

"And that is why I suggested it," Edward replied bluntly. "M'mother will know how to take Miss Delwyn in hand and introduce her about even if she is betrothed to you."

"Ought I to take that as an insult?" Jeremy asked his friend evenly.

"How can you?" Edward retorted. "You've spent the last eight years doing nothing but trying to prove you're the wildest fellow in London. It ain't your fault you didn't succeed. But to complain to me now of your reputation would be the outside of enough!"

"I have been wild, haven't I?" Jeremy said thoughtfully. "Well, my father is determined to change that and I begin to wonder if perhaps he isn't right."

"Here, here!" Hastings said in mock alarm. "You ain't sick, are you? Feverish, p'rhaps? Next you'll be telling me you mean to wed Miss Delwyn after all."

Jeremy laughed harshly. "You forget, she has already refused me. Not that I am not grateful for the escape. I need no such determined woman about me; far better that I should find someone biddable whom I can leave behind in the country and who I may be sure will not interfere with my pleasures."

"Oh, certainly," Hastings agreed dryly, "and never mind the boredom."

"Enough," Jeremy said in a dangerously quiet voice. "You've made your point and we are almost at White's. Do try to recollect our purpose tonight."

As the two young men entered White's they immediately found themselves surrounded by Jeremy's friends. They were, without exception, heedless rakes and gamblers and miscreants.

"Jeremy!" one of them called out, his voice showing the effects of more than a little wine. "To be leg-shackled at last, are you?"

"Did you hear of Ware's latest scandal?" someone else said, trying to avert a fight.

"Care to wager on the race to Brighton to be held next Wednesday, Barnett?"

With something akin to dismay, Jeremy realized that there was not a one among them he could have introduced to Emmaline with pride. With unaccustomed curtness he excused himself from their company, saying, "Sorry, my friends. I am pledged to respectability for the next few months. Certainly until after my nuptials. And if you have been wagering that the notice in the *Gazette* was an error, have a care to your pockets."

Amid good-natured curses, Barnett and Hastings moved on into another room of the club. Edward only had time to murmur, "You lie very well," before they were met with frosty stares.

More than one member of White's had been heard to state that Jeremy Barnett ought never to have been admitted to the club. Still, one or two came forward, if a trifle reluctantly, to wish him well. "Congratulations, Barnett. I own I am astonished to hear you are to wed Delwyn's daughter," Lord Alvanley said, a note of interest to his voice.

"Thank you, m'lord," Jeremy replied coolly, refusing to say more.

Another member said bluntly, "I trust you will not be offended, Barnett, if I say that the girl deserves far better than you."

"How can I be offended when I quite agree?" Jeremy replied with a simper.

Recognizing the signs of his friend's rising temper, Edward intervened hastily, "That's as may be, Jeremy, but the young lady appears to consider herself fortunate."

"The more fool she!" another member snorted.

Jeremy raised his quizzing glass to his eye and spoke grimly. "Ah, Crandall, but that is precisely where you are out! The last word one might use with respect to Miss Delwyn is *fool*. And may I remind you that I am her fiancé and that I might take grave exception to any slur cast upon her character?"

Both men stared at one another, neither willing to give way. In exasperation Hastings told Jeremy, "Oh, do give over! They will meet Miss Delwyn soon enough and see for themselves. You do her a discredit when you act as though she cannot speak for herself."

Jeremy turned to his friend and demanded wearily, "Why is it that I tolerate you, Hastings? You are most unlike my other companions."

"Praise God for that!" Edward replied coolly. "As for why you tolerate me, you have no choice. Miss Delwyn is staying at m'mother's house, remember?"

"Your mother's house?" Petersham demanded.

Suddenly everyone's interest had been aroused. Mutters of "That makes a difference, indeed!" could be heard in the background.

As though unaware of the whispers, Hastings replied calmly, "Come, Jeremy, I believe we are engaged to play cards this evening. And before that I wish to dine."

Arm in arm, the two friends left the room apparently oblivious to the consternation they left behind. They did not, however, in the end play cards. Instead, after more than enough wine, Jeremy Barnett angrily dragged his friend along to a certain house in St. John's Woods. "Are you sure this is wise?" Hastings asked doubtfully. "If your father—"

"My father is precisely the reason we are going there," Jeremy said coldly. "Even he would not expect me to give up my mistress without telling her so myself."

"Give up your mistress?" Hastings choked. "Here, I say, isn't that going a bit far?"

Jeremy met his friend's eyes coolly. "As I told Miss Delwyn, I mean to give my father no cause for complaint in the next few weeks. And he would have complaint were it to get out and about I was visiting my mistress while Emmaline was in town. Besides," he said with a wry smile, "my current situation no longer allows of my paying Daphne's expenses. It is only fair to free her to take on a protector who can. What about you, Edward?"

Hastings looked affronted. "No offense, old fellow, but you know I've never much liked the woman. Delightful as she is, of course."

Jeremy bowed ironically. "Any further objections?" he asked.

"None."

"Good. Do you mean to accompany me, then, or will you leave me to face her, er, temper alone?"

"Oh, very well, I'll come with you," Hastings grumbled good-naturedly. "Though mind, only if you do indeed mean to break with her."

"I do, Hastings, I do," came the maddeningly calm reply.

8

WORD soon spread that Jeremy Barnett's fiancée was in London and staying with Mrs. Hastings. That lady, never a recluse, found herself inundated with callers, all curious to see her young houseguest. It was a circumstance she accepted with great equanimity.

"It is only human nature," she told Emmaline calmly. "Just as it is human nature to be spiteful should they find anything in you to dislike—so have a care, my dear. Not that I think you need worry. It is also human nature to be delighted to see such a fellow as Jeremy Barnett captured at last. Besides, if you recollect all that I have taught you these past few days, the *ton* should find nothing to fault in you."

Which was no more than the truth, Emmaline thought wryly as her maid put the finishing touches to her toilette and she prepared to go downstairs. Mademoiselle Suzette had done a superb job in outfitting Emmaline for her comeout, and both Mrs. Hastings and Jeremy were doing their best to polish her manners for the *ton*—not that those manners had required a great deal of polishing.

Still, she knew herself to be at her best as she descended the stairs. She wore a sprigged muslin gown and her hair done up charmingly by Mrs. Hastings' own hairdresser and an air of modesty that belied her knowledge of the reason most visitors had come to call.

Jeremy was, of course, already there. He had no wish to court his father's ire by appearing to neglect Emmaline, particularly not before his own plans were resolved. But to ensure that, he must ensure her acceptance by the dragons of the *ton*. So each day, as Mrs. Hastings received her visitors, he called and sat with Emmaline, the perfect embodiment of a reformed rake. More than one matron went away voicing her distrust of Barnett's transformation, but none could deny that at the very least Miss Delwyn had coaxed such a pretense out of the young man and that was a thing most would have been prepared to wager was impossible.

More than that, a friendship began to grow between the counterfeit couple—albeit an uneasy one. In the quiet afternoons Jeremy would take Emmaline to visit parts of the city most members of the *ton* were scarcely aware of. More than one almshouse and hospital had reason to thank him for his generosity, as did a number of individuals. And after his initial disbelief that she was truly interested, he allowed Emmaline to help him in his endeavors. For Emmaline, they were a welcome change from the frivolous mornings, which, while entertaining, seemed strangely empty after the years of taking care of her father. And Jeremy could not deny that her caring concern meant as much to many of these people as his money. Still, she could not bring herself to marry him.

After one particularly tedious morning and discouraging afternoon, both Jeremy and Emmaline escaped to go for a drive with something akin to relief. She wore a gown of very becoming creamy silk with lace at the bosom and wrists, a fetching creation of straw upon her head. Jeremy wore a coat of blue that fitted him superbly, as always, over pants of the lightest shade of brown. They made, more than one observer noted, a very handsome couple.

Neatly he threaded his curricle through the crowded streets and into the park. As usual when he was in London, Jeremy drove mismatched horses, a conceit that was but one more way that Jeremy thumbed his nose at the conventions of the *ton*. Sporting men knew, however, that in spite of their appearance, these horses were among the fastest goers in London and that Jeremy Barnett possessed an enviable skill with the whip.

None of these things was on Emmaline's mind, however, as she twisted the fabric of her skirt in her hands. Unaware of her unusual distress, Jeremy continued with his lecture. "Upon no account must you waltz at Almack's until you are given permission. You are fortunate as it is to receive cards admitting you, but Edward knew his mother would somehow contrive. I suppose we must thank the Countess Lieven. She has always disliked me intensely and it is her way of saying she is delighted I am to be leg-shackled at last."

"How gratifying to know that my acceptance is

based upon my ability to discomfort you," Emmaline replied, goaded by these words.

Jeremy drew his horses to a halt and turned to look at Emmaline in astonishment. "Now that is the most hen-witted thing I have ever heard! As if you didn't know very well that my current acceptance is due almost entirely to your patent virtues." Emmaline shrugged and, exasperated, Jeremy went on, "I should think you might have the grace to at least appear grateful for the efforts I am making upon your behalf. I have introduced you to no less than five very respectable, very eligible young gentlemen. And with luck you will soon have your pick of a great many more. All acceptable to your father and mine."

"Oh yes, they were respectable indeed!" Emmaline agreed, her eyes flashing. "And all five of them without two thoughts to rub together between them."

Aghast at what she had just said, Emmaline covered her mouth with one hand. In spite of himself, Jeremy laughed and once more urged his horses forward. "Well, but you cannot blame me for that," he told her with a grin. "You claim to be so respectable yourself that I thought you would like them."

"Hmmm," Emmaline agreed warily. "As though I didn't know very well that you are worried about what your father will say when we break off our betrothal. You wish to see me settled with someone he would approve of."

This was familiar ground. Once more Jeremy risked a glance at Emmaline. "Someone you and your father would approve of," he corrected her grimly. "Somehow I find that matters more to me than what my father will think of the fellow. How is your father? What news do you have of him?"

Emmaline looked down at her hands and spoke with some difficulty. "Mrs. Colton, writes that he is doing well but I cannot help but know she is trying to spare me worry. I have lived too long with Papa's illness to believe he will recover. But at least I am reassured there are no new crisis."

"And did you write your father about London?" Jeremy asked, a trifle anxiously.

In spite of herself, Emmaline smiled. "Yes, yes I did. And Papa wrote back that he is delighted I am enjoying myself. He says that even in the shires word has reached him of the success I am having. He also says that word has reached your father of your reformed behavior and Lord Barnett is more confirmed than ever in his belief that our betrothal was a good thing. Papa says he is still pressing for an immediate wedding but he has persuaded him to wait a little longer."

"Thank God for your father's good sense!" Jeremy said savagely. "Were matters left to mine, we would have a disaster upon our heads."

Emmaline placed a gentle hand on Jeremy's arm. "I cannot think your father means you ill," she said. "Too often I have heard him speak of you with gruff affection, for all the anger that was in his voice as well."

Biting off each word as he spoke, Jeremy said, "My father has always hated me. I cannot doubt that if he could, he would have me unborn. Were it possible, he would disown me entirely and I him. Instead you and I are forced to this masquerade, and I am sorry you must play a part in it. You would have been better off had you never known my father and me."

Quietly Emmaline withdrew her hand. "Indeed?" she asked with a sigh. "Have you forgotten that I accepted you of my own free will? Or that I agreed to this plan to please *both* our fathers? To be sure it was a mistake, but you can scarcely claim all the blame yourself for our mutual folly."

"It is pointless to argue with you, isn't it?" he asked with a laugh.

"Certainly it is if you intend to wallow in self-pity," she replied bluntly. "So let us speak of other matters. I think I may have someone you will like."

Jeremy groaned. "Another demure chit, straight from the schoolroom?" he demanded.

"That is not entirely fair," Emmaline said frostily. "I have also pointed out to you two widows, both just shy of four and twenty."

"Aye, and both have thrown their caps at me before," he told Emmaline grimly. "I don't like them nor would my father."

"Shall I look among the demimonde, then?" Emmaline asked sweetly. "I had thought of it, knowing your preference for their company, but the thought of your father held me back. After all, had that been acceptable, you would long since have chosen Daphne," she said, throwing out a name she had overheard coupled with his, hoping he would deny it.

But as usual, Jeremy did not do as Emmaline wished. Instead, he once more halted the horses and turned to her, his face full of thunder. So angry was he that he grasped her wrist with his hand as he roared, "By the devil! Is this the effect a betrothal to me has had on you? Surely Mrs. Hastings, if no one else, has told you that my mistresses are none of your affair. You know very well you ought never to think of such things much less speak of them, particularly to me. I ought to . . ."

Her heart pounding with rage and jealousy, Emmaline spoke more defiantly than she meant to. "You ought to what?" she challenged him with smoldering eyes.

And there, in the park, in full view of the *ton*, Jeremy kissed Emmaline, pulling her to him angrily and pressing his lips down on hers punishingly. To his astonishment and her own, she found herself once more giving in to the insistence of his caresses, her own hands stealing around his neck as his stole around her waist. All the hours that both of them had spent assuring themselves this would never happen again dissolved as if they had never been. Only the restlessness of his horses pulled Jeremy back to his senses. As he fought to get them under control, Emmaline leaned back, coloring, as she became aware of the amused stares of passersby. Too late, pride came to her rescue as she demanded furiously, "Why did you do that? It will only make our betrothal the harder to break!"

Angry himself, Jeremy did not at once reply. Instead, he settled his horses, then urged them forward at an extremely sedate pace before he said coolly, "Don't worry, Miss Delwyn. With my reputation it will be assumed that I forced myself upon you and have given you a distaste of me. Though I must say that your own response will make that a trifle hard to swallow. Are you trying to imitate Daphne? I assure you, you cannot match her skill!" He paused, then said very deliberately, "If you are so determined to be rid of me, my dear, I suggest you curb your wayward nature or you may have no choice in the matter. Neither of us will."

Emmaline blushed hotly, her anger fanned by his reference to his mistress. She forced herself to speak calmly, however. "We cannot break off the betrothal at once, in any event. Our agreement is that we would not until you had found an alternative partner. Unless ... has your solicitor said there is a way around your father's conditions?" she asked eagerly.

"Until *we* had found alternative partners," Jeremy reminded her irritably. "And no, Nicholson tells me there is no way around them. The estate is entailed in such a way that I am completely at my father's mercy."

"I see." Emmaline leaned back with a sigh. A trifle grimly she said, "I must confess that your settlement seems to me a greater priority than my own. After all, we need merely tell him I broke the engagement for my own reasons."

"And your father?"

"My father will understand, if he is still alive to care. I shall make him understand," she told him resolutely. "But you are changing the subject."

"If you are waiting for me to say I am sorry I kissed you, then I must tell you I will not," Jeremy replied with maddening calm. "I quite enjoyed myself and would not mind doing so again. And it is quite evident you felt the same. I don't expect you to admit to that, however, since you insist upon having taken me in such dislike. As to your reputation, should someone have the poor grace to mention it, you need merely freeze the person with a stare and he or she will begin to think themselves mistaken. Agreed?"

"Agreed," Emmaline replied coolly.

"Good." He paused, then added high-handedly, "But I think we had best look about us for a husband for you, whatever your protests. If you are this warm-blooded with someone you say you dislike, you had best have someone to bed you whom you can marry," he told her ruthlessly. "Unless you are of a mind to marry me after all?"

"Never!" she retorted. Then, with a scornful laugh she added, "Why? Does your father press harder for an immediate resolution? Are your creditors hounding you at your door?"

"You appear to give very little credence to my proposal," Jeremy said, lips white with anger.

"Pray, pardon me, sir," Emmaline said with exaggerated courtesy, "for doubting you. Why, after my experience with your *honesty* in such matters, I must be all about in my head to question your motives. Perhaps you are genuinely tired of looking about you for a wife and have decided that I must do, after all. Kind sir, I am overwhelmed by your flattery! No, Jeremy, I think we had best stick to our plans and find you another bride."

For a long moment he did not speak. Then, curtly he said, "Well? Are you going to tell me who it is you have found for me?"

"Have you ever met Rosalind Kirkwood?" Emmaline asked, eager to change the subject. "I know she has been absent from London this Season because her youngest sister was ill, but now she has returned. I thought you might have already met her, however, because she was brought out three years ago."

Barnett frowned. "Kirkwood? Yes. A quiet girl, so far as I recall, but not an altogether unattractive one. Have you been introduced to her?"

"More than that," Emmaline replied with a smile. "Rosalind and I were best friends at school. She has a fine mind, good conversation, some wit, and general amiability. Your father would certainly like and approve of her and yet she is less likely to bore you than most of the girls you will find in London this Season. No doubt she will be at Carlton House tomorrow night."

"You have convinced me," Jeremy said gallantly. Emmaline regarded him with distinct suspicion, and after a moment, he added teasingly, "To meet her, at any rate, and speak with her."

"You won't fall in love, I expect," Emmaline said with a shrug, "but it is the best I can do. And there are reasons that I think she might not be entirely averse to your suit."

Once more Jeremy drew his horses to a halt and placed a hand over hers, this time comfortingly. "I don't expect passion," he said. "My father has made it clear that I am past the point where I may be so choosy. No, I only look for a solution to get us both out of this tangle my father has placed us in. And to find a woman whose face I will not come to hate over the breakfast table and who will not come to hate mine. I admit to some surprise, however, that your friend is unmarried, if she is as delightful as you say."

Emmaline chose her words carefully. "Rosalind is prone to . . . to shyness, but in spite of that she does not lack sense."

"Nevertheless, her family ought to have seen to finding her a husband," Jeremy pointed out with a frown.

"And so they should have," Emmaline replied tartly, "if Lady Kirkwood were not so fond of having a daughter about upon whose shoulders she could lay the responsibility for running the household and whom she could turn to for company. Why do you look so doubtful? Lady Kirkwood is, after all, only following the lead of the Queen."

"I see," Jeremy said grimly. "The girl is so far past her prayers that she would marry anyone. Unless, of course, she has had her head filled with nonsense and expects romance and a hero to sweep her off of her feet."

"Rosalind is not addicted to novels, if that is what you mean," Emmaline replied severely. "Nor does she confuse life with what is to be found between the covers of a book." She paused and a wry smile twisted her lips as she said, "You need not fear. Unlike me, Rosalind is an eminently sensible young woman. I cannot count the number of arguments we used to have at school. I held that marriage ought only to come with love and she argued that not only was I foolish but naive as well. She held that were the two people personable, intelligent, and civilized, any pair might make a go of marriage. She will not chide you for having mistresses," Emmaline could not resist adding bitterly.

"Well then," Jeremy said briskly, "we must hope that our apparent betrothal does not rule me out in her eyes. I shall look to you for help with that. Otherwise she sounds admirable for our purpose. A pity I am such a bad bargain for her."

As Emmaline's face softened in distress he added curtly, urging his horses forward again, "Nor do I want your pity, thank you Miss Delwyn. Look to your own future for that!"

He could not know what effort it cost her to smile. Suddenly the day seemed grim at the notion of Rosalind and Jeremy together and she wished the words unsaid. Last night, when she had thought about the matter, Emmaline had been clear-headed. Rosalind was the perfect choice, if she was not to marry Jeremy herself. And she would not. But that was before he had kissed her. And now it was too late.

Back at Mrs. Hastings' town house Emmaline discovered two more letters waiting for her, this time from her sisters. Caroline was concerned that Emmaline should be enjoying herself so heedlessly in London while neglecting their father at home. She did allow, however, that Mrs. Colton was taking good care of Sir Osbert. Too good care, Emmaline could almost hear her sister sniffing. In the other letter Adeline scolded Emmaline for having her name bandied about so freely among the *ton*. As she had said before Emmaline left for London, she felt it improper and immodest of Emmaline to expose herself to *on-dits* instead of quietly marrying Jeremy Barnett. Indeed, she did not see the necessity of Emmaline making a London comeout at all. After all she and Caroline had not displayed such vanity.

In spite of herself, Emmaline could not entirely suppress a sigh. If Adeline considered it improper of her to have come to London, what would she say if she knew what had occurred in the park today?

"Trouble, my dear?" Mrs. Hastings asked briskly from the doorway of the drawing room.

Emmaline started at the sound of her hostess's voice. She delayed a moment in turning around. After all, what could she say? She had no doubt that Mrs. Hastings would be appalled if she knew how far beyond the pale Emmaline had put herself with her behavior. In the end she prevaricated.

"Only my sisters reminding me that it is my duty to be at my father's side," Emmaline replied with apparent frankness. "A duty I fear I am sadly neglecting."

"Nonsense!" Mrs. Hastings retorted stoutly.

"I wish I could be certain," Emmaline smiled sadly. "However, I will not argue with you any more than I will argue with my father."

"Are you enjoying London?" Mrs. Hastings asked, a trifle anxiously.

"To be sure." Emmaline forced herself to laugh. "And that is part of my guilt."

"Well, since you are here," Mrs. Hastings said briskly, "it is absurd to regret your good fortune, for then you will have wasted it."

On impulse Emmaline rose and walked over to her hostess. "You are kind," she said. "And I am very fortunate to be your houseguest."

"So you are," that redoubtable lady agreed. "And

to further regret your presence here in London is to insult me as a hostess," she decreed imperiously.

"And that I could not do!" Emmaline agreed with a laugh. "Very well, I shall cease to mourn and go upstairs and consult with Mary as to what gown I should wear tonight to the theater."

9

IN the end it was Hastings who met Rosalind Kirkwood first. Emmaline had risen early after a night filled with half-remembered dreams. Her restlessness communicated itself to Edward over the breakfast table and he asked if there were any errands he could run for her. He had already heard a garbled version of what had occurred in the park from someone who had seen the pair and he now drew his own conclusions.

Emmaline paused as she was about to lift a forkful of food to her mouth. Resolutely she set the fork down and said, "Yes, if you would, Edward. I should dearly love to go to Hookham's Library this morning, and your mother is still abed. I very much fear she would scold me if I went alone."

"I am entirely at your service," he told her with a gallant smile.

Emmaline's own smile was warm in return. "How fortunate I am that you are Jeremy's friend!" she murmured.

"And I that you are his fiancée," he retorted.

They bantered back and forth awhile before

Emmaline ran upstairs to retrieve her reticule and gloves and hat. In a morning dress of green muslin she looked delightful. A short time later, they were on their way in Edward's phaeton. As he threaded his way through the busy streets, more quietly but just as skillfully as Jeremy, he said carefully, "I hope you will not think me impertinent, Miss Delwyn, but I feel I must speak. Jeremy is a good fellow and I would not see him hurt for the world. I'll grant you he is a trifle wild and his father had good reason to be angry. Indeed, I find myself angry with him as often as not. But he is a good fellow at heart."

Emmaline hesitated, then decided upon frankness. "I do not doubt it, Mr. Hastings. My father has always had a high regard for Mr. Barnett."

"Then why—"

"Why did I end the betrothal?" Emmaline asked coolly.

He nodded. "It has me in a puzzle, for I cannot think you truly dislike Jeremy as much as you say you do. In the past weeks I have often wondered . . ."

She looked down at her hands clasped together tightly in her lap. "Can you not see?" she demanded. "It is as much for his sake as mine! Every time anyone speaks of our wedding he flinches from the course and goes quite pale. It was even worse before we came to London. Did you think I could not see his reluctance to the match?" She stopped and met Hastings' gaze squarely. "Was I to ignore his feelings, and my own uncertainties? Would it have been a kindness to marry him when he did not truly wish it? Even if he were mad enough to accept such a union, I could not. I have too clearly my own sister's example before me." Emmaline stopped, aghast at her own frankness. "F—forgive me," she stammered, "I ought not to speak of that, it is a private matter."

"I am all discretion," Hastings said with quiet sincerity. "Still, as I understand it, you will not repeat your sister's mistake," he suggested quietly, "for Jeremy's sake as well as your own?" She nodded and he went on, "But what if you are mistaken about his feelings?"

"Do you tell me I am?" Emmaline countered, afraid to hear either answer.

Hastings was the first to give way. "I do not know," he admitted quietly. "Indeed, I think Jeremy does not know his own mind on this."

"Well, I cannot decide his for him when I am not even certain of my own," she replied tartly. "I only know I cannot marry Jeremy as matters now stand."

Hastings read the resolution upon her face and sighed. "Would that all young ladies had your strength of character, Miss Delwyn. Assuming you are correct, of course, about Jeremy. He is not a man to be easily satisfied with half measures. But enough of that. We are at Hookham's Library."

As he spoke, Hastings neatly drew his horses to a halt and gave the reins over into the care of his groom before he helped Emmaline descend from the phaeton.

Inside, as Emmaline looked about her at the shelves of books, Edward stayed by her side, apparently not in the least rush to leave. He was perfectly willing to discuss the merits of the books she selected and made no demur at the suggestion of a cup of tea to refresh themselves.

It was as they were about to leave the library, rather reluctantly, that Emmaline heard her name called and they turned to see a young lady standing quite close to them. She was, Hastings thought, the most beautiful young lady he had ever seen. She was almost precisely the same height as Emmaline but as fair as Miss Delwyn was dark. Golden curls peeked out from under a blue silk bonnet that matched precisely the blue silk gown the young lady wore. "Emmaline!" she repeated happily. "Mama told me you were in town and I came straight back from my uncle's house to see you. When did you arrive? How is your father? I have so missed you and I cannot bear the thought that my sister Lizzie's indisposition has kept me from London and seeing you these past few weeks. My dearest friend, I have heard you are engaged to Jeremy Barnett and I shall want to hear all about it and why you never wrote to tell me."

At Hastings' discreet cough at her elbow, Emmaline found a way to break into her friend's flow of words. With a laugh she said, "Well, if you know all that, then you know I am staying with Mrs. Hastings. May I present her son, Edward? Edward, this is Miss Rosalind Kirkwood, my very best friend in school."

Hastings bowed and Rosalind blushed very prettily. The three exchanged a few more words and then a loud voice called out, warningly, "Rosalind! We must be going."

A shadow crossed the girl's face and those nearby gentlemen who had been watching her with approval suddenly found themselves wondering why they had ever thought her pretty. Her head bowed, Rosalind to Emmaline in a whisper, "Do you go tonight, to Carlton House? Good. Then we'll meet there and find a way to talk. You must help me."

Thoughtfully Emmaline watched her go, acknowledging with a false smile the brief nod Lady Kirkwood sent in her direction. Beside her Edward Hastings stood quite still and Emmaline had to speak to him twice before he heard her. Outside, in the phaeton, he could not keep from asking, "What the devil is the matter with that girl? Why isn't she married yet? And why does she go so dreadfully gray when her mother speaks to her?"

Stiffly Emmaline replied, "There is nothing the matter with Rosalind. It is not her fault that her parents dislike every young gentleman who has ever came to call. Indeed, until this year I thought they never meant her to marry at all. But of a sudden I hear they wish her to consider marriage to a fellow to whom her father owes gambling debts!"

"Good God, the poor girl!" Hastings said with feeling.

"Yes, that is why—"

Abruptly Emmaline broke off, causing Edward to look at her suspiciously. "That is why, *what*?" he demanded.

Edward's face darkened so alarmingly that something compelled Emmaline to reply with a careless shrug, "That is why I hope she may find someone else."

It was a very silent pair that returned to the

Hastings town house to find Jeremy there waiting for them. A trifle stiffly, Edward excused himself and left Emmaline to tell Jeremy about their morning.

Mrs. Hastings did not miss the look in her son's eyes when he returned from his outing with Miss Delwyn. There was an air of abstraction about him that she had never seen before as well as a smile that alternated with a grim look of disapproval that played about his lips. Her own tightened at the uneasy suspicion that Edward was halfway to falling in love. It was, nevertheless, some time later in the day before she had the opportunity to question her son about the matter.

"Ah, Edward, there you are, my dear," Mrs. Hastings called cheerfully up to her son as he stood on the stairs. "Wait a moment, will you? I must speak to you."

"Certainly, Mother," he replied with impeccable manners.

Unaware of her thoughts, he amiably followed her to the small library that was usually his father's preserve. Even now the aroma of tobacco lingered among the crowded rows of books that so badly needed straightening. Mr. Hastings, however, was nowhere to be seen. Once there Mrs. Hastings seemed to have some difficulty speaking and Edward prompted her politely. "Is something wrong, Mama?"

"Oh, no, no," she replied airily. "At least I don't think so." She paused, then added lightly, "Is Miss Delwyn enjoying her visit to London? Did you have a good morning today?"

Unaware of it himself, Edward's face lit up as

he said boyishly, "Oh, yes, indeed! We went to Hookham's Library and it was wonderful!"

With great self-restraint Mrs. Hastings refrained from asking tartly just what could be so wonderful about a library, even for a son who enjoyed books. Instead she said, "I suppose we are soon to hear the date set for her wedding to young Barnett? Particularly if the reports I hear of her behavior— *their* behavior—in the park yesterday are to be believed."

"Well, er, no," Hastings told his mother reluctantly. "I rather think we shan't. As for those reports, I am persuaded they are much exaggerated."

"I see," Mrs. Hastings said, quirking an eyebrow. "You are satisfied with the state of affairs then?"

Again Edward's face darkened. "No, to be frank I think Jeremy is treating Miss Delwyn abominably!" he said angrily. Then, hastily he added, "Not that I think Miss Delwyn is so eager to wed him, as matters now stand. And I shouldn't allow her to be pressed against her will."

With something akin to dismay, Mrs. Hastings watched the emotions that played across her son's face. It was no part of her plans to have him defend Miss Delwyn so forcefully. Coupled with the air of abstraction she had noted before, Mrs. Hastings was afraid that her son had indeed begun to fall in love. Unable to suppress her curiosity, she asked, with a feigned coolness, "Edward, you must know that I have begun to wonder if you ever intend to think of marriage or if you mean to become a misogamist like Jeremy Barnett."

Edward's easy laugh only added to her dismay

as he replied, "Have no fear, Mother. I know my duty, and today I begin to think I may even take pleasure in it. But now, unless you have something urgent to say to me, I must go. I am pledged to run an errand for Miss Delwyn straightaway."

10

CARLTON House. It seemed incredible to Emmaline that she should actually find herself going there. To be sure, Edward had told her that his mother had been one of the Prince of Wales's flirts in her salad days and since her marriage such invitations to the Hastings had not been uncommon.

This, however, was not an ordinary occasion. Although the Allied Sovereigns had already left England, Prinny had had the happy notion of celebrating the Duke of Wellington's return instead. Even those members of the *ton* who had left London were returning for this affair.

Indeed, Emmaline could not help but feel that Mrs. Hastings had worked miracles in prompting Mademoiselle Suzette to have their ball gowns ready in time. Half of London, it seemed, required the same thing. Emmaline's gown was of white satin with an overdress of silver lace. With it she wore white gloves and silver slippers, with diamonds about her throat and dangling from her ears. "A young girl's colors," Mrs. Hastings had admitted, "but the cut of the dress is not and on you the contrast is stunning."

Her own gown was a triumph of blue damask

satin and lace, and the clear sapphires she wore
were a perfect complement to the dress. Edward,
Mr. Hastings, and Jeremy were already waiting
downstairs to escort them to the ball when Emmaline and Mrs. Hastings finally pronounced themselves ready. The two younger gentlemen bowed
deeply to the two ladies and Emmaline felt a catch
in her throat as she thought how handsome Jeremy looked tonight. Nor did she detect anything
other than complete admiration in his eyes as he
took her hand in greeting.

Mr. Hastings contented himself with clearing
his throat and saying to his wife, "Well, well. As
usual you shall outshine all the other ladies there,
my dear. And Miss Delwyn, I've no doubt that
seeing you just now, young Barnett thinks himself
a very lucky fellow indeed."

Coloring in confusion, Emmaline curtsied to her
host, afraid to meet Jeremy's eyes. It was one
thing to think him handsome, another to contem-
plate the madness of a lifetime wed to the man.

Edward, noting Miss Delwyn's high color and
his friend's look of suppressed anger, hastily said,
"Yes, we all look marvelous, but now it is time to
be going. We are not so important that the Prince
Regent will forgive us for being terribly late!"

Mrs. Hastings was not a stupid woman. She had
not missed Emmaline or Jeremy's reaction to her
husband's words, nor even Edward's. So her son
was worried over the girl's feelings, was he? All
very commendable and gentlemanly, no doubt,
just so long as his concern did not cross over into
more than that. She had no wish for Edward to
develop a *tendre* for Emmaline; she had far more
ambitious plans for him than that. Still, she sec-

onded him ably. "Edward is quite right. Let us be off at once."

Later Emmaline would remember being utterly overwhelmed at the sight of Carlton House and at their reception. Over two thousand guests were expected, Edward told her, beginning at nine P.M. It was later than that when the Hastings party arrived and their carriage waited in line some time before it was their turn to descend. They were received at the grand entrance by equerries who led them to the garden, where they were presented to Prinny. He wore, Jeremy explained to Emmaline under his breath, a field marshal's full dress uniform complete with medals.

The festivities had evidently put Prinny in a good mood, for he expressed himself delighted to welcome the Hastings party and even congratulated Emmaline upon her betrothal to Jeremy. How he knew about that was beyond her and she could only curtsy deeply as Prinny told Jeremy playfully, "It is to be hoped you will be more fortunate than the Prince of Orange!"

At least that was what Emmaline thought he said. Her head was in such a whirl that it was not until they had moved away and begun to look about at the banks of flowers and the covered walkways and the Corinthian temple with its bust of Wellington that Emmaline began to feel herself again. "Such an honor!" Mrs. Hastings was saying, a trifle breathlessly. "Townsend must have told him of your betrothal, but even so, such an honor!"

"And one that I could do without," Jeremy muttered grimly to Emmaline. "It will make things all the more difficult."

"Can it matter?" Emmaline murmured. "Surely you have never formed one of his circle anyway?"

"No, but your father once did," Jeremy retorted. "And for all his unpopularity, I should not care to have the Prince Regent declare me or you *persona non grata* at court."

It was no surprise than that Rosalind spotted Emmaline first, for that young lady was more accustomed to such affairs than Emmaline. Nor had she just faced the unwelcome congratulations of her prince. Lady Kirkwood did not look pleased when her daughter insisted that they join the Hastings party but she did not object. Particularly when Jeremy suggested they go to the dance pavilion.

Once more Emmaline felt overwhelmed as they entered the huge polygonal building. The ceiling looked to have been draped with muslin, and had Edward not told her it was merely painted so, she would never have known. There were mirrors on the walls, draperies, chandeliers, and banks of artificial flowers that hid the musicians. Clearly Prinny had spared no expense, but then, Mrs. Hastings said dryly, he never did.

Emmaline was grateful that her friend was more composed than she was just then. It was Rosalind who smoothed the way for both parties to continue to spend the evening together. She was respectful to Mrs. Hastings and a trifle shy with the gentlemen. To be sure, Lady Kirkwood merely looked on, an habitual frown fixed upon her face, but she did not protest when Jeremy asked her daughter to dance and Rosalind readily agreed. Rather, she took it as something to be expected. After all, Rosalind was a Kirkwood.

That left a somewhat startled Edward with the obligation to ask Emmaline. "Bad form," he told her as he led her onto the floor. "Jeremy ought to have asked you, his fiancée, to dance first."

"Yes, but I'm not really engaged to Jeremy," Emmaline objected.

"Doesn't matter," Edward said stoutly. "Everyone thinks he is and he ought to behave as if he were." He paused and smiled down warmly at Emmaline. "If I were Jeremy, I know I should have asked you first. Indeed, I shouldn't be looking about me at all; I should be quite content to honor my betrothal."

"And were I betrothed to you, I should scarcely be so eager to break those vows," Emmaline replied kindly.

Returning to his sense of anger, however, Edward added, "It is the outside of enough for Jeremy to ask Miss Kirkwood to dance."

"But I wished him to," Emmaline said. At his startled look she added, "Don't you recall? I said I wished Rosalind to find someone else to wed, and who better than Jeremy? He *must* find a wife and Rosalind will not bore him."

"Yes, but will he please her?" Edward muttered.

Mrs. Hastings watched as her son and Emmaline danced. She could not hear the words they spoke, of course, but she did not like the expressions that crossed her son's face. He ought to betray nothing more than mild contentment when he danced with a young lady. Why anyone watching would think he and Emmaline were upon intimate terms with one another!

Jeremy also noted the interchange and to his surprise felt anger rising in his breast at the sight of Emmaline and Edward in such evidently warm conversation. When the dance ended, he contrived to be virtually at their sides. "My dance next, Miss Delwyn, I believe," Jeremy said in a voice that brooked no refusal.

Emmaline accepted without demur, eager to learn what he thought of Rosalind. Meanwhile, ever the gentleman, Edward asked that lady to dance. It was a duty, however, that he scarcely found distasteful.

"Did you enjoy yourself with Edward?" Jeremy demanded curtly as they danced.

A trifle puzzled, Emmaline replied, "Yes, of course I did. And you Rosalind?"

"She is a delightful girl," Jeremy allowed handsomely. "But I take leave to warn you to have a care with Edward."

The figures of the dance separated them then, and when they came together again Emmaline said warily, "What did you mean about Edward?"

"Just what I said. He is an amiable fellow, ever ready to make himself agreeable to the ladies, but that is all. His mother, however, is another matter. She is as eager to keep him from a wife as my father is to find me one. She will take the least hint of friendship between you as a pledge of betrothal and try to warn him away. Edward might be fool enough to think he ought to defy her."

"Indeed?" Emmaline asked frostily. "You appear to have very little faith in your friend's intelligence. But even if you are right, I should think you would be pleased if that occurred. Wouldn't it ease your worry over my father?"

"I should not like to see you or Edward make a

fool of yourselves" was all Jeremy had time to reply before they were separated again.

After that dance, Emmaline was amused to note that Mrs. Hastings and Lady Kirkwood were deep in amiable conversation. Neither lady paused to do more than briefly acknowledge the return of the two young women before continuing with their gossip. Meanwhile Rosalind noticed that an unwary partner had stepped on the hem of Emmaline's dress.

"Never mind," Rosalind said intently, "I shall show you where you may pin it up."

And with that the girl drew Emmaline away from her chaperon.

As one who had visited Carlton House before, Rosalind had no trouble finding a quiet room where she quickly helped Emmaline repair the damage to her dress. Then she rose to her feet and sighed, "How I envy you," she said. "Here in London on your own and free to do as you wish."

Emmaline could not entirely suppress a bitter laugh. "I assure you it scarcely seems so to me! Mrs. Hastings keeps as sharp an eye on me as any mother could, and so does my fiancé. I am as hemmed in by convention as any other young lady and have not even the freedom of being in my own house."

"But you have the prospect before you of marriage and the freedom that goes with that. Marriage to a gentleman who is not a source of distaste to you. Indeed," Rosalind countered, "your future seems a most desirable one."

"Do you think so?" Emmaline asked impulsively. "It is true I have known Jeremy almost all my life

and think the world of him, but of late I think we
have both begun to wonder if we should suit."

Rosalind frowned thoughtfully. "He has, to be
sure, an unenviable reputation, but more than
one rake has been steadied by marriage."

"Not this one, I fear," Emmaline replied, a trifle
shakily.

"Still, he will one day inherit a title and a respectable estate, one that you will be mistress of,"
Rosalind pointed out shrewdly. "If he is not the
man you once dreamed of, nevertheless you could
do far worse." She paused, then added dryly, "Unless I am mistaken, however, he is in fact the man
you once dreamed of wedding. Or so you told me
when we were at school together. Have you
changed in your feelings?"

Emmaline evaded the issue. Turning away so
that her friend could not read her face, she said
sharply, "I have never been as practical as you,
Rosalind. However advantageous the match, there
are reasons I do not wish to marry Jeremy Barnett. Reasons that you or someone else would not
feel."

"I see," Rosalind replied slowly. "So you do mean
to end the betrothal. That will not be an easy
thing to do. How will you manage it? And how
did you come to be betrothed in the first place?"

Emmaline started at the sound of footsteps in
the passage outside the room. "We cannot talk
freely here," she said. "I will come and see you
and we may talk then. I shall explain everything."

Rosalind nodded. "I should like that. Mama keeps
me so sheltered that sometimes I feel I shall go
mad with boredom and loneliness. But come. We
had best return to the dancing. My mother and

Mrs. Hastings will be wondering what has become of us."

In perfect accord and arm in arm the two young ladies retraced their steps.

Jeremy was waiting impatiently. As soon as he spied the two young women he crossed the floor to his fiancée. "Come, Emmaline, dance with me," he ordered imperiously.

As she did so, Emmaline found herself wondering, not for the first time, what would come of this counterfeit betrothal.

In the end, it was a long night for the Hastings and Kirkwood parties. The Queen did not sit down to supper until 2 A.M., and it was some time later before they did. And although she left at four-thirty in the morning, it was past dawn before the rest of the guests departed from Carlton House. Indeed, in the carriage on the way home, Emmaline was heard to mutter that she would be delighted if she never danced again. Jeremy only laughed.

11

To the surprise of everyone, Jeremy arrived in time to share breakfast with the Hastings family two days after the fête at Carlton House. After greeting everyone politely and seating himself, he turned to Emmaline and said, "I know you are pledged to call upon Miss Rosalind this morning and I came to escort you. Perhaps Edward would care to come as well?"

Edward had expected the question and meant to refuse. The thought of watching Jeremy attempt to fix his interest with that superb girl appalled him and he did not think he could bear it. But the look of grim determination upon his friend's face and the knowledge that, in the end, he could not bear not to see what transpired, changed his mind. With a careless shrug Edward said, "Oh, yes, of course, if you wish it."

"Splendid!" Mrs. Hastings said graciously. "I am so pleased to see you young people enjoying yourselves. Emmaline, my dear, have you had any further word from your family as to how your father is doing?"

"Only the usual," she replied, a trifle sadly. "No

doubt Mrs. Colton is taking the most excellent care of Papa but I cannot help but worry."

Mrs. Hastings patted her hand. "Never mind, my dear, I should not have asked. I am certain, however, that if there were cause for alarm, your family would summon you home at once. Indeed, you have said yourself that that is their promise."

Jeremy coughed discreetly. "My father mentioned in *his* letter that your father seems a trifle better since you've left," he said. "And you well know he is not given to exaggeration."

At this point Mr. Hastings, who greatly disliked discouraging talk at the breakfast table, intruded. "Come, come, enough of this. I should like to hear what Emmaline thought of Carlton House, for I have not yet had a chance to ask her. It is this wild, gay life you are all leading, of course."

A short time later all three young people were riding in Jeremy's curricle toward Rosalind's town address. "Now why the devil did you drag me along?" Edward asked his friend with ill-concealed irritation.

Favoring Edward with a withering look, Jeremy explained, "Because, you shatter-brained fellow, I have decided that Miss Rosalind will have to do. I cannot say I have fallen madly in love with her, but she is better than the rest of the crop, I suppose. At any rate, time is slipping away and I must choose someone."

"I should think you already had," Hastings muttered. At the dagger glances thrown at him by the other two Edward said, "Oh, very well. So you've decided you shan't suit but that Miss Rosalind will do. What has that to do with me?"

"You are indeed feather-witted today," Jeremy

repeated with no little exasperation. "Surely you must see that I cannot openly court Miss Rosalind while I am supposed to be betrothed to Miss Delwyn."

"Certainly," Edward agreed. "That is why it is so convenient that Miss Delwyn is a friend of hers."

"Yes, but don't you see?" Jeremy asked winningly. "A far better cover for my interest would be if you were to pretend an interest and the four of us could be seen about without arousing any comment."

"Any comment save that *I* have developed a *tendre* for her," Edward countered scathingly. "That is not precisely to my liking."

"But there will be no harm done," Jeremy wheedled. "In the end I shall marry her and you will be held blameless and one can scarcely say she will be harmed in any way."

"Yes, but what if she should take my intentions seriously?" Edward protested. "Or her mother?"

"You need not fear," Emmaline said quickly. "Rosalind is already aware that my betrothal to Jeremy is not so firmly fixed as it seems. We may safely tell her the truth."

"And her mother?" Edward asked warily.

"Her mother will come around. If need be we shall present her with a *fait accompli*," Emmaline said blithely in her innocence.

She would not have been so sanguine could she have heard the discussion between Rosalind and her mother going on at that moment.

Rosalind was in her room dressing. Her mother dismissed the maid and began to help her daughter herself. "The Marquess of Alnwick has returned to London, my dear," she said briskly. Oblivious to her daughter's sudden pallor, she went on, "He came and spoke to your father while we were at Carlton House and I am happy to tell you that he said all that is proper."

"Wh-what do you mean, Mama?" Rosalind asked tremulously.

"Well what should I mean?" Lady Kirkwood asked in exasperation. "He asked permission to court you, of course. And to marry you."

"What did you tell him?"

"Nothing! I have already told you he spoke to your father. Honestly, Rosalind, sometimes I think you have the wits of a peagoose!"

"Papa, then. What did he tell Alnwick?"

"He told him yes. Do you think your father is such a fool as to ignore what a triumph such a match would be for you?" Lady Kirkwood asked impatiently.

"But—but I dislike him," Rosalind found the courage to protest.

Lady Kirkwood dearly wished to shake her daughter but was clever enough to reply instead, "Now, now, child. You have always been a sensible creature. You know we will not force you to any-thing, but we do wish you to be aware of the advantages of the position you would hold as his wife. Love always seems attractive at your age, but it does not last, I assure you. A sensible match works far better. As for your professed dislike of the fellow, that is mere maidenly nerves. You ought to be flattered that your future husband looks at you with such becoming warmth."

Lady Kirkwood paused and regarded her daugh-ter shrewdly. After a moment she shrugged and said lightly, "We will not press you, for the moment, Rosalind. The Marquess of Alnwick departed London almost as abruptly as he arrived. He does not return, I understand, until the first of August. You have until then to accustom yourself to the notion. When he arrives, however, he intends to speak to you himself and he will have to have an answer. I need not say that we expect it will be a favorable one, need I, Rosalind?"

The girl avoided her mother's fixed stare. "No, Mama," she said quietly.

At that moment a knocker sounded downstairs and a few moments later one of the servants arrived to announce that Miss Rosalind had callers. "We shall be down straightaway," her mother said briskly upon hearing the names. "Mr. Barnett is spoken for, of course, but Mr. Hastings is not."

"I thought you wished me to marry the Marquess of Alnwick," Rosalind said with some surprise.

"I do," her mother agreed. "But it does no harm for him to see that you are admired by other gentlemen as well. We may hope for a larger settlement that way."

Having concluded her maternal advice, Lady Kirkwood gave her daughter a slight push toward the bedroom door. Rosalind did not resist.

Half an hour later the three guests took their leave. A tentative plan had been made for the four young people to go to the park together the next day and Lady Kirkwood had raised no objection. She meant what she said about obtaining a larger settlement from the marquess.

Hastings, on the other hand, once they had dropped Emmaline off at home and he was alone with Jeremy, had a great many objections. "I cannot go with you," he said curtly. "I have other plans tomorrow, and despite what you said before you shall have to make my apologies to Miss Kirkwood and depend upon Emmaline for your excuse to see her."

Frowning, Jeremy pulled his horses up short and paused to give his friend a searching look. After a moment he said, as curtly as Hastings, "This is not the place to talk about such matters. We shall go to my lodgings and discuss this over a neat luncheon."

"I am not hungry," Hastings retorted.

"You will be, my friend, you will be," Barnett assured him enigmatically.

True to his word, as soon as they had reached Jeremy's rooms in St. James and seen to the horses and he had removed his gloves, Jeremy gave orders to his man for something to eat. Then, pouring his friend a glass of wine, he said, with something of a twinkle in his eye, "Very well, Edward, now you may tell me everything and I promise to listen to it all. And don't spare my feelings I pray you, for I shall know it if you do."

After a long moment, Edward rose to his feet with a snort. "Very well"—he echoed Jeremy's words—"I shall. I refuse to help you entrap Miss Kirkwood into marriage, Jeremy. Nothing will prevail on me to do so and it is only our deep friendship that makes me stand aside and allow you to do this at all. But I swear, Jeremy, should I ever hear that you have made her unhappy . . ."

In astonishment he broke off at the sight of Jeremy laughing. "Are you mad?" Hastings demanded incredulously. "What the devil do you find to laugh about in this fiasco?"

"Forgive me," Jeremy said, controlling his laughter, but with a pronounced twinkle still in his eyes. "I did not mean any disrespect to you or Miss Kirkwood. Indeed, it is just that all of this suits my plan perfectly."

In anger Hastings turned away. "What plan?" he asked roughly over his shoulder.

"My plan to wed Emmaline and for you to wed Miss Kirkwood" came the astonishing reply.

Immediately Edward whirled around. "But you said—"

"I said a great many things in Miss Delwyn's presence that I did not mean," Jeremy replied curtly. "It is no part of my plan for her to know what I am about."

Somewhat calmer now, Hastings took his seat and once more sipped from the wineglass. A twinkle now danced in his eyes as he said with a deep sigh, "All right, you reprobate, tell me what you are about. Though my warning concerning Miss Kirkwood still stands. I will not have her hurt."

"Nor do I mean to hurt her," Jeremy said gravely. "Had I not seen how you looked at her and she at you at Carlton House and again today and had I not been told the story of her expected betrothal to a certain notorious marquess, I should not have hatched it at all."

He paused and Hastings demanded impatiently, "Well?"

"Well, my dear Edward," Jeremy said, lazily swinging the ribbon that held his quizzing glass, "I mean for the four of us to go out and about, just as I said when we were with Emmaline. She is to believe the Banbury tale I spun then. The truth, however, is that you will deepen your acquaintance with Miss Kirkwood with a view to your future and hers."

Edward frowned. "I like that part well enough," he agreed, "but what of your future? And Emmaline? If I am not mistaken, she has refused to marry you."

Again there was a long pause as Barnett minutely inspected his boots before replying, with the same lazy drawl, "Miss Delwyn, my dear Edward, is going to change her mind even if I have to kidnap her to make her do so."

"What the devil!" Hastings was once more upon his feet. "You must be mad."

Jeremy appeared to give the matter much thought. "I don't think so," he said judiciously.

"Are you foxed, then?" Hastings demanded suspiciously. "Or are you roasting me? You know very well Miss Delwyn does not wish to marry you and is unlikely to change her mind. At least not so long as she knows you don't have a *tendre* for her. Or do you mean to lie to her?" An awful suspicion occurred to Edward and he asked, "You're not doing this out of pique, are you? Because she didn't immediately fall into your arms the way most young women do?"

A dark look crossed Jeremy's face as he asked bitterly, "*Et tu*, Edward?" Long acquaintance with that look warned Hastings to be silent and after a moment Jeremy went on, "That is precisely why I do not court Miss Delwyn directly, my dear friend. She would no more trust my motives than you do. But somewhat to my surprise, Edward, I find I have fallen in love with her. Oh, to be sure, when my father first proposed the match I was hotheaded and angry and in no mood to be pleased with what I found. Instead of the meek little mouse I intended to lock away in the country each year, I found someone who could match me at every turn and who could never be so easily disposed of. And I readily confess I was not very successful at hiding my feelings from her. But now . . . now, Hastings, I find I don't want a mousy little creature. I want someone precisely like Miss Delwyn. Only she will not have me."

"And do you believe you will make her a suitable husband?" Hastings asked impudently. "You've spoken a great deal about what will please you but have you given a thought to what would please her?"

"I have," Jeremy replied coolly. "Emmaline's not some milk-and-water chit, content to play propriety all her life. She has too much spirit for that and needs someone who will love her as she is and not always be telling her that she must guard her tongue or her actions."

"And you think that kidnapping her will change her mind? Or this—this absurd charade will do the trick?" Hastings demanded impatiently.

"I mean to make her love me," Jeremy said, meeting his friend's eyes squarely. "And yes, I quite believe I can. I was jesting about kidnapping her, but a little jealousy may do wonders. You will no doubt disapprove of me, Edward, when I tell you this, but I have kissed Emmaline and there was neither indifference nor dislike in her response. Only a fear of trusting me, I think."

"Yes, I know. In the park," Edward grumbled. "But I cannot believe you think more deception will change distrust to trust," he added incredulously.

Jeremy sighed heavily. "No. I am in hopes that time will change her opinion of me as she sees that I am not the hopeless wretch she thought I was. Or that she will finally stop fighting her feelings for me. Dammit, Edward, do you think I like this plan I have set forth? If there were any alternative, I would take it! But the girl is too eager to find me another bride and will not consent to simply let me woo her."

"Why not tell her your solicitor has found a solution to the problem," Hastings asked reasonably, "and that you are wedding her out of desire, not need."

"Because he has not and she would soon find that out," Jeremy replied bitterly "Moreover, if I said he had, Emmaline would return to her home tomorrow."

"Why not simply tell her the truth then," Edward asked. "As you have told me today."

"Because she would not believe me," he answered quietly. "Even you did not. She would think my father pressed me for the wedding and that I was once more lying to her to meet his demands. Under such terms she would never marry me for her pride is damned near as strong as my own. No, I have thought about this and only if she believes I have an alternative will she accept the notion that I do wish to marry her of my own choice. Will you help me? Or have I mistaken your feelings for Miss Kirkwood?"

"You have not mistaken them," Edward conceded reluctantly. "And I confess I have no wish to see her wed that fellow the Marquess of Alnwick. Or to you. Very well, I shall do as you ask."

Jeremy clapped his friend on the shoulder. "You

are the most excellent of fellows, Edward! And I promise that I shall take great care that Miss Kirkwood does not fall in love with me. Not that I have much fear of that after seeing how she looked at you," he said. "All right?"

In answer, Edward said gruffly, "Where the devil is your man with our lunch?"

12

IF Hastings was uncomfortable with the plan, Emmaline was even more so. Not that she knew what Jeremy was about, but the more she thought about it, the more distressing she found the notion of Jeremy wedding her friend Rosalind. It would not be fair to her friend, she told herself stoutly, and that was surely the reason for her discontent. On the other hand, marriage to Jeremy would surely be better than marriage between Rosalind and her marquess, wouldn't it? Several mornings later, thoroughly miserable, Emmaline prepared for her friend's visit.

So did Edward, taking great pains with his appearance so that he was a quarter of an hour late coming down to breakfast, a fact that did not escape his mother's notice. "Edward," she said with deceptive lightness, "I wonder if you would be kind enough to escort me about this morning. I have some errands I must run and need your assistance."

"Take m'father," he answered promptly.

"I cannot. He is pledged to friends," she replied evenly.

"So too am I," Edward said with a set look to his jaw. "I am pledged to spend the morning with Miss Delwyn and her friend Miss Kirkwood."

The faint flush that accompanied this statement caused Mrs. Hastings' own blood to rise, but she was far too subtle a woman to speak her thoughts openly. Instead she laughed artfully and said, "Well, of course if you do not trust Barnett to watch after them . . ."

"I do not," he answered firmly. Then, with a loyalty to Jeremy that cost him dearly he added, "Surely you must see, Mother? You know how matters stand between Emmaline and Jeremy. He wishes to court Miss Kirkwood and must have my presence as a cover to his intentions."

"Indeed, I see everything," Mrs. Hastings said grimly. Then, forcing herself to laugh again, she added, "Very well. I hope you have a happy morning, the four of you. I shall somehow manage on my own."

Her anger was so great that Mrs. Hastings entirely failed to see how cast down Emmaline was at Edward's words. If she had, it might have gone a long way toward setting her fears to rest. Edward was not so blind. After his mother had gone, he turned to Emmaline and asked, with no little concern, "Is something wrong?" She shook her head and he added with a heartiness he did not feel, "Our plans are going splendidly, you know. Why, I have no doubt that in a few weeks all shall be settled between Jeremy and Miss Kirkwood for a wedding forthwith."

And why that should give her an instant headache was more than she could understand! Emmaline told herself tartly. Aloud, however, she only said, "Yes, splendidly. I suppose he really does care for her?"

A twinge of conscience made Edward pause, but resolutely he pressed on with Jeremy's plan. Possessing himself of Emmaline's hand, he assured her falsely, "You need have no fear, Miss Delwyn. Soon you will be free to return home to Selborne, if that is what you wish, and Jeremy will never trouble you again."

It was the look of utter bleakness that crossed her face then that reconciled Edward to Jeremy's intentions. In spite of himself he asked her, "Have I distressed you, Miss Delwyn? Am I mistaken and do you wish to marry Jeremy after all?"

At once Emmaline sprang to her feet and turned her back to him. Over her shoulder she flung at Hastings, "M—marry Jeremy? Don't be absurd! I have told you before we should not suit. Particularly now that I know he has formed a—a *tendre* for someone else."

"And if he had not?" Edward persisted. "If he had formed a *tendre* for you?"

Now she rounded on him. "How dare you roast me like this?" she demanded angrily. "You know very well that while I amuse him, Jeremy can, at times, scarcely abide my presence. It is no kindness in you to pretend otherwise."

"Suppose Jeremy were to say otherwise?" Edward asked meekly.

Emmaline laughed mirthlessly. "Oh, in that event I should know that Jeremy had despaired of having Rosalind's hand in marriage and that with his father hard at his heels he had decided I must do after all. Not that he would say so. No, for all his faults, Jeremy is too much the gentleman to admit such a thing. He would know all the right words to woo me but I should not be so foolish as to believe him a second time, I promise you! Now pray excuse me, I have some things I must do before Rosalind arrives."

And with that Emmaline escaped upstairs. Or thought she had escaped. Instead she found Mrs. Hastings waiting for her in her room. That lady was pacing the floor and appeared to be in a state of some agitation. Emmaline was all concern. "Has anything happened?" she asked at once.

Mrs. Hastings looked at her young houseguest squarely. "Not yet, my dear," she said frankly, "but I fear it soon shall. I feel as though I have utterly failed you."

Somewhat taken aback, Emmaline blinked as she said, "Failed me? Whatever can you mean, ma'am?"

This time it was Mrs. Hastings who possessed herself of Emmaline's hands as she said, "My poor child, do you think I do not know what it will mean to you should Barnett marry Miss Kirkwood instead? Oh yes, yes, I know you say that is your wish as well, but have you truly considered the gossip it will give rise to? However much you may concur in his decision, the *ton* will see only that he threw you over for someone else. And that is a thing no one can like." She paused and regarded Emmaline steadily as she said, "Do you truly dislike young Barnett so much? Has he offended you so horribly?"

Emmaline blushed. Avoiding those searching

eyes, she said, "Didn't you once say that no one would hold me to blame were I to call off the betrothal?"

"No one other than Prinny," Mrs. Hastings allowed frankly. "However, this is another matter. It will look as though he overthrew you. I ask you again, do you hate Jeremy Barnett so deeply?"

Emmaline did not mean to allow her face to betray her. And had she not been so tired, no doubt her training would have stood her in good stead and she would have succeeded in deceiving Mrs. Hastings. But as it was, Mrs. Hastings took a breath of satisfaction and said kindly, "My dear, you cannot hide from me that you have a fondness for Jeremy and that the notion that he will wed someone else is making you desperately unhappy."

Emmaline kept her eyes firmly fixed anywhere but upon her hostess as she replied, a trifle breathlessly, "You cannot know that. And even if it were true, what is that to the point? It alters nothing."

"It alters everything, *if* you possess the slightest resolution," Mrs. Hastings answered tartly. "Marry Jeremy yourself. At once, before this nonsense with Miss Kirkwood goes any further."

In vain Emmaline tried to pull her hands free. "I cannot! I will not marry a man who is indifferent or dislikes me. Not—not when I love him."

Mrs. Hastings let go of her guest's hands. "You are so certain of how he feels then?" she asked with raised eyebrows.

"Yes!"

"So?"

"So?" Emmaline repeated, a trifle dazed. "What do you mean?"

"I mean that I think you something of a little fool!" Mrs. Hastings said tartly. "To tamely watch the man you love marry someone else because he does not love you is the height of folly!"

"But I could not bear to love him so dearly and see him every day indifferent to me," Emmaline cried.

"I should think not," Mrs. Hastings agreed coolly. "No one is asking you to. But I would think that had you the slightest resolution you would at least make a push to alter matters."

"Alter matters? How?"

Mrs. Hastings sighed in exasperation. "My dear Emmaline, I had no notion you were such a peagoose! Though perhaps it is not your fault. The lack of a mother's hand these past five years and more has certainly done you no service. What I mean is that I expect you to make a push to cause the fellow to love you. Surely his attentions are not so firmly fixed upon Miss Kirkwood that that is impossible?"

"No," Emmaline agreed coolly. "What makes it impossible is that Jeremy has taken me in dislike. He is forever dressing me down for one imagined fault or another and telling me how thoroughly he disapproves of my behavior."

"That does not sound like indifference to me," Mrs. Hastings said with raised eyebrows.

"No, it is dislike, and that is far worse," Emmaline retorted crossly. "He has not even tried to kiss me since the day before he met Rosalind, nor shown any jealousy since the ball at Carlton House."

Mrs. Hastings, who had chosen to speak to Emmaline more out of desperation than from any sense that matters could be truly altered, became both thoughtful and steadily more cheerful. After a silence that could not help but grate upon Emmaline's sensibilities, she said quietly, "So, my dear, he has kissed you? How often?"

"Twice," Emmaline said pettishly. "No, three times. But that means nothing. Jeremy is a hardened rake and no doubt steals a kiss whenever he can find one."

Mrs. Hastings did not trouble to hide her amusement. "My dear child," she said, "Jeremy may be a rake but one can scarcely call him hardened, as yet. As for stealing kisses: with the demi monde, yes, as often as he is able. But for all his faults, the boy is a gentleman and he would scarcely kiss someone as gently bred as yourself lightly. Perhaps there is hope yet. Particularly if you tell me he was jealous."

"Well, I do not see it," Emmaline countered.

"That is because you are still a child in such matters, whatever your true age may be," Mrs. Hastings said amiably. "You have had no one to explain things to you and I have been remiss in not doing so since you came under my roof."

Still unconvinced, Emmaline asked her hostess crossly, "Very well, ma'am. What do you say I am to do?"

Mrs. Hastings did not immediately answer. Indeed, the silence stretched on so long that Emmaline once more began to despair. At last, however, her hostess said briskly, "We need not concern ourselves about your wardrobe. That is already bang up to the mark and flattering to you besides. You have made a start in stirring the flames of jealousy, and a touch more of that cannot hurt. Show yourself willing to be pleased by the courtesies shown you by other gentlemen. Allow Jeremy to become angry with you, but never you with him. Indeed, you must be all cool dignity or, should he deign to scold you, meekly obedient. Surprise him, confuse him, make him doubt his own mind about you. Learn to flirt discreetly." A thought occurred to her and she added suspiciously, "Miss Kirkwood is, I believe, a friend of yours, is she not?"

"Yes," Emmaline admitted unwillingly.

"Good. Then you may confide in her and ask her help," Mrs. Hastings said briskly. "She may be alternately hot and cold with Jeremy and so outrageous in her demands of his time and proof of affection that he will turn in relief to someone as sensible as you shall prove yourself to be."

Then, allowing no dissent, Mrs. Hastings rose to her feet, shook out her skirts, and continued in the same brisk tone, "Look to it, my girl. As for me, I truly do have errands I must run. But I shall nevertheless contrive to arrange it that you have a chance to speak to Miss Kirkwood alone, up here in your bedchamber, before my son or Jeremy sees her. For we shouldn't want Edward to know what we are about; he might warn Jeremy. You wait here and make yourself as attractive as you can. My dresser must do your hair in some new manner. I shall attend to everything. And remember, my dear, resolution is all that is wanted here. Follow my advice and we shall have you wed to Jeremy before August is out. I ought to know, as I've married off a daughter and three nieces with not a spinster left in the family."

Then, pausing only long enough to kiss Emmaline affectionately upon the cheek, Mrs. Hastings was gone, leaving her young houseguest to anxiously consult the looking glass and ring for her maid.

13

MRS. Hastings was true to her word. Her dresser knocked on Emmaline's door scarcely five minutes after that lady left her. With nimble fingers and numerous observations about foolish young women who neglected to use to advantage the skill of those about them, she set to work on Emmaline's hair.

Rosalind was shown up to Emmaline's room just as Miss Canfield finished. Both girls waited until she had left before they threw their arms about one another. Then Rosalind asked anxiously, "What is it, Emmy? I was told I must come up to you at once. Are you ill? Has something occurred? Have you . . . have you heard from your father or about him? Is he—"

Hastily Emmaline stemmed the flow of words. "No, Rosalind. I swear, nothing of the sort has occurred."

Rosalind regarded her friend with narrow eyes and asked suspiciously, "Emmaline, are you up to mischief, again? At Mrs. Winfred's School you used always to get just such a look before you engaged in some sort of nonsense." Then her voice altered entirely as she laughed and said, "Tell me what it is and what part I may play!"

Emmaline laughed, a trifle ruefully. "You may not wish to play a part when you know what I am about. Indeed, you may wish me at Jericho and prefer to let matters continue as they have begun."

"Well, unless I know what you are talking about, how can I judge the matter?" Rosalind asked reasonably as she sat on the chair by Emmaline's dressing table. "Why don't you tell me everything?"

An innate reluctance to expose her own foolishness to anyone as well as a lack of opportunity had heretofore prevented Emmaline from telling Rosalind the circumstances of her betrothal to Jeremy. Now she did so, leaving out nothing of her own feelings or his reaction to questions of setting a date. She even told her friend the plot that had brought them to London and the part she had imagined Rosalind might play. Then Emmaline paused, wishing to discover Rosalind's reaction to the notion of marrying Jeremy.

Rosalind all but jumped to her feet and began to pace the room. Her words tumbled over themselves as she tried to explain how she felt. "I had not thought . . . He is so entirely the gentleman, and he has been so kind in his attentions . . . Mama would be so distressed . . . I had somehow though Mr. Hastings . . . Of course I cannot bear the thought of marriage to . . . to . . . Anyone must be better than him and truly I can think of no one else who might marry me . . . But Jeremy was betrothed to you and I did not think . . . Although you did say . . . But what about Mr. Hasting? I thought he—"

In confusion Rosalind broke off and laughed at herself. "Look at me," she said a trifle grimly. "Wasn't I the one who always preached to you that one must be sensible about marriage and not look for passion? That one must always keep one's wits about one? It would be sensible to marry Mr. Barnett since I cannot bear the Marquess of Alnwick, but I find, unaccountably, that I wish rather to know about Mr. Hastings."

Emmaline looked away, embarrassed. "Edward is merely to keep the tattleboxes from wondering what we are about," she said with real regret. "You see, we thought it would not do for them to realize that Jeremy means to wed someone else."

"Oh," Rosalind said quietly. Then, taking a deep breath, she said, "Very well, you have told me all about your betrothal, as you promised you would. But I still do not understand. What is it you wish me to do?"

"I am not entirely certain," Emmaline replied hesitantly. "Mrs. Hastings has guessed that I am not indifferent to Jeremy. She said that between us you might push Jeremy away and I draw him closer, but I cannot bear to think you may be forced to wed Alnwick."

A trifle pale, Rosalind answered resolutely, "It shall not come to that, I promise you."

"Oh, and how will you prevent it?" Emmaline demanded tartly. "You've never had the resolution to stand up to your parents before, and even if you did so now, how could you disobey them? You've no money, no other family to flee to, how could you run from them? For I've no doubt they would make your life unbearable if you did not."

Rosalind took another deep breath before she

replied, "I shall depend upon you, then. Or you and Jeremy, for perhaps by then you will be wed."

"And if I am not?" Emmaline asked hollowly. "If in spite of Mrs. Hastings advice, he does not wish to marry me but clings to the desire to marry you?"

"If there is no chance he will marry you then . . ."

"Then you will marry him if he wishes it," Emmaline decided for her friend. "You have said that you like him, and if there is not love, at least it will be a civil marriage and your heart will not ache that you share a bed and home with a man who does not love you in return. Agreed?"

Rosalind swallowed. "Very well," she said resolutely, although her voice wavered. "If, in the end, Jeremy will not marry you but does wish to marry me and my parents are pressing me to wed the Marquess of Alnwick, and . . . and there is no one else, then I shall marry him. But not, mind you, if there is the least doubt about any of those three things."

Impulsively Emmaline hugged her friend. "You must, you know," she told Rosalind stoutly. "For Jeremy's sake as well as your own. He has to marry and soon." Rosalind hesitated before answering and Emmaline pressed her, "What is it? What troubles you?"

Rosalind met her friend's eyes steadily as she said, "All of this. When we were in school together, before your father became ill, you were used to talk of Jeremy as though he were perfect. Then, when Mama brought me out, I saw a rather different view of him. Now, well, all this seems—"

She broke off in confusion and Emmaline smiled

wryly, "Strange? Mad perhaps?" she suggested. "I suppose it does. But if he loved me, I think I would be very happy wed to Jeremy. He laughs at the same things I do. We used almost to be friends and sometimes in these past few weeks I have felt we were again." She paused and an odd light came into her eyes. "Do you know, he goes about making certain that various charities do not lack for funds? And champions individuals who have fallen down on their luck? Helps them to find a place again? It is not a side of him I had expected to find, I confess, and yet I did, here in London."

"I have never heard that said of him," Rosalind observed quietly.

Emmaline shook her head. "No, you would not. I had the devil of a time even getting him to let me come along on some of his expeditions. Sometimes I think he'd rather the world thought him an ogre. Oh, Rosalind, don't you see? I would never need fear that he would bore me with his predictability or respectability, for he doesn't care for such things any more than I do. You, of all people, Rosalind, know how often Mrs. Winfred scolded me for recklessness and unconventionality. You know how much I have always chafed at my skirts and all the rules that hem women about. The years have taught me prudence, but I shall never care for prim propriety. So you see, it would be fatal for me to marry a man who would assume and expect that I did! Jeremy would take me as I am. If he loved me."

A look of distress settled upon Rosalind's face, and seeking to banish it, Emmaline said briskly, "Enough! Come along. It is time we went down-

stairs. I've no doubt Jeremy and Edward are waiting for us."

In point of fact, the two men were laying their
own plans and broke off hastily at the sound of
the two young ladies descending the stairs. His
face carefully expressionless, Edward watched as
Jeremy went up to Miss Kirkwood, possessed her
hand in his own, and said warmly, "How delightful to see you, Miss Kirkwood. It seems forever
since I last had the pleasure of your company."

In spite of herself, the young lady giggled. "It
was just yesterday, Mr. Barnett, in the park," she
told him sternly.

His eyes dancing, Jeremy retorted, "There, you
see I told you it was forever!"

Rosalind blushed, then mindful of Emmaline's
advice to blow both hot and cold, she turned
to Edward and said with uncharacteristic warmth,
"Mr. Hastings. How nice to see you again."

That gentleman bowed gravely and said with a
smile and quiet sincerity, "My dear Miss Kirkwood, it is always a pleasure to see you."

Hastily Emmaline possessed herself of Edward's
arm and looked up at him warmly before greeting
her fiancé coolly. "Hallo. You are looking a trifle
tired today, Jeremy. A long night, I fear?"

"No longer than Edward's," he answered shortly.
"And may I tell you, Emmaline, that I take exception to the way you are clinging to my friend? It
would not be the thing even if you were not officially engaged to me. Such impropriety might well
give the fastidious cause for gossip."

Forgetting all her resolutions, Emmaline retorted
hotly, "Ah yes, you cannot bear I should embar-

rass you, is that not so? At least I do not flaunt my mistresses in the park when everyone is about!"

For a long moment there was an appalled silence in the room as Jeremy carefully studied the impeccable manicured nails upon one of his hands. Then, meeting her eyes directly, he said calmly, "Nor have I, my dear, since our betrothal was announced. You really must learn to eschew such vulgarity. I have told you before I dislike these references to such women. Need I repeat the lesson?"

As Emmaline recalled just what he had done the last time, she turned a deep crimson and would have fled had Edward not said softly, "Courage, Miss Delwyn."

Instantly her back straightened and her chin came up. Jeremy merely laughed and turned to Rosalind. "Pray forgive us our wrangling, Miss Kirkwood. I've no doubt that by now Emmaline has told you the truth of our betrothal, and while I have no wish to have that knowledge bruited about, I know I may trust in your discretion. Come, let us go into the library. There are some books there I think you would like to see."

Helplessly Emmaline watched them go, unaware that beside her Edward was hard put to suppress a smile. His face was impassive, however, as she turned to him and said tartly, "Jeremy does not appear to know how to go about wooing my friend. If he imagines such a scene as just passed will do him a service in her eyes, he is much mistaken!"

Edward could not very well tell her that Jeremy was in fact taking great care to ensure that Miss Kirkwood did not fall in love with him. Instead he said with apparent concern, "Do you think it wise,

Miss Delwyn, for us to allow them to go unchaper-
oned? Mightn't it be better for us to join them at
once."

Stricken, Emmaline agreed with alacrity. "Yes, it
will do Rosalind's reputation no good for it to be
bruited about that she has been *tête-à-tête* with my
fiancé."

If there was a bitterness in the last word, Edward
did not remark upon it. Instead he quietly led the
way, merely commenting on how lovely her friend
looked that morning. His quiet talk, however, gave
way to a fit of coughing when, upon opening the
library door, they discovered Jeremy standing far
too close to Rosalind for propriety as he solicitously pointed out a passage in one of the books,
one hand resting lightly on her shoulder. With an
expression that Emmaline could only interpret as
great self-satisfaction, Jeremy met her eyes and
said coolly, "Hallo. Come to join us, have you?"

Only Rosalind appeared to notice the look of
dismay that Emmaline could not control and, blushing, she hastily moved away from Jeremy. Her
own cheeks flushed with anger, Emmaline said
evenly, "May I speak with you alone, Jeremy? In
the drawing room, perhaps?"

"I am at your service," he answered with a half
bow.

Emmaline contained her temper until they were
once more in the room filled with Egyptian furniture. Today the absurdity of it did not amuse her
at all, and when he had closed the doors behind
them, she rounded on Jeremy and demanded angrily, "How dare you treat my friend that way?"

"I do not recall that she objected to my manner," he answered coolly.

As though to further annoy her, Jeremy crossed his arms over his chest, leaned against the wall, and watched as Emmaline paced about the room. "You know very well what I mean!" she flung at him. "If Rosalind is too inexperienced to know that you have gone beyond the line then you are not! I said you might court her, not ruin her or cause her the least distress."

"I have no intention of ruining Miss Kirkwood," Jeremy protested innocently. "My father shouldn't accept her as a bride if I did. As for distress, why life is never entirely free of that, is it?"

Emmaline paused in her pacing to face him then. "The devil take you, Jeremy Barnett! Don't roast me like this, I mean what I say. Rosalind is not some doxy of yours to be treated so carelessly."

At that Jeremy's eyes narrowed and he came away from the wall, advancing menacingly upon Emmaline. "I have told you before such words are not becoming in my fiancée," he said dangerously, "and whether you like it or not, you still are my fiancée."

"What—what are you going to do?" Emmaline asked faintly as she came up against a sofa and could retreat no further.

"This!" he exclaimed as he caught her to him.

One hand went around her waist and pressed Emmaline against the length of his body, the other forced her head back and her face up to meet his. Then, before she even had time to form a protest, Jeremy's lips were upon hers, once more punishing and demanding. To her horror, the hand on her waist left it to begin to tug at the top of her dress, then reached inside to fondle her breasts. As Emmaline turned scarlet, she tried to pull free, but the hand tangled in her hair held fast and she could not, though her struggles caused Jeremy to lift his lips from hers. A gleam of amusement lit his eyes as he looked down at her flushed face.

"Like it, my dear?" he asked sardonically. "*This* is how one treats a doxy!"

"Let me go or I'll scream!" Emmaline whispered, now very pale.

His face only a few inches away from hers, Jeremy laughed. "Scream? And have the servants come running to witness your position? I think not, my dear."

In despair, Emmaline knew he was right and she once more tried to twist free. Jeremy merely pulled sharply on her hair and Emmaline knew she was still caught. Once more he lowered his lips to hers, this time more slowly and more gently. Insistently they played at hers until, helplessly, she swayed toward him and her lips parted, a wave of longing threatening to drown her. No longer did she try to protest the hand that played so deliciously with the nipples of her breasts, nor did she even notice when the hand left her hair to find its way down her back and press her hips against his. So lost was she to all common sense that her eyes were still closed when he thrust her from him and Emmaline did not at once realize what he was about.

For a moment she swayed, then, startled, opened her eyes. Jeremy, she saw, was once more leaning against the wall, arms crossed over his chest, eyes hooded. There was no trace of discomposure in his voice, she thought bitterly, as he said, "That, my dear Emmaline, is how one treats a doxy and I will thank you not to say that what I do with Miss Kirkwood is in any way the same."

Trembling slightly, Emmaline turned her back on him, struggling to regain her own composure. "No?" she flung over her shoulder. "If you have treated me this way, how can I know you will not treat Rosalind the same?"

Jeremy laughed softly before he replied. "But my dear Emmaline, I am not yet betrothed to her as I am to you. I realize I am regarded as something of a rake but even I must draw the line somewhere."

Then, somehow, treacherously, he was at her shoulder, his hands upon her waist and his lips brushing the nape of her neck as he went on, teasingly, "Besides, Emmaline, I scarcely imagine Rosalind would respond to me as you have done, encouraging me to go so far with her. You really must learn to restrain this wayward nature of yours before it lands you in the briars." One hand reached upward absentmindedly to stroke her trembling shoulder as he added, maddeningly, "Unless, of course, it is just me that you respond to and you wish to resume our betrothal after all? I am sure I could procure a special license; we would not even need to wait the three weeks while the banns were read. What do you say, my love?"

Furious, her eyes full of tears, Emmaline once more pulled free of him, hating the aching desire for his touch that still coursed through her. Beyond caring, she hurled angry words at Jeremy. "Don't ever touch me again! I know very well how you hate me and I wouldn't marry you if you were the only man in England! Indeed, I am quite resolved upon spinsterhood. It would be far preferable to marriage to a man who likes nothing better than to torment me as you do!"

Then, blindly, she fled the room, not seeing the look of dismay that came to his face or the way he would have followed her had the appearance of a footman in the hallway not forestalled him. Nor did she know how, cursing himself for a fool, Jeremy fled the Hastings household not five minutes later, leaving a bemused Edward and Rosalind to entertain one another.

14

EMMALINE spent a good many hours trying to decide how she could face Jeremy when next she saw him. She need not have fretted for he did not visit again for several days. Aware that something had gone wrong, Mrs. Hastings discreetly tried to question her young houseguest but was met by silence. Only with Edward did Emmaline appear to feel at ease, a circumstance that did not escape his mother.

At any rate, when Jeremy did appear, not by the slightest gesture or word did he betray any recollection of what had last occurred between them. Indeed, when he arrived to escort Emmaline to the theater, his first words after he greeted her were, "You are certain Miss Kirkwood knows we are to meet her there?"

"Yes, of course. Edward has already gone to collect her," Emmaline replied with creditable composure.

Only then did he pause, inspect her coolly, and say with maddening calm, "You look a trifle peaked. Have you been getting sufficient rest, Miss Delwyn?"

As Emmaline choked, Mrs. Hastings said tartly, "That is none of your affair, since I gather you do not really intend to marry her. I do suggest, how-ever, that tonight you contrive to appear to pay some mind to your fiancée, Barnett, otherwise everyone will be saying that it is your neglect that has caused Emmaline to be out of looks."

Jeremy's eyes narrowed speculatively a moment before he nodded. Disingenuously he said, "What an excellent notion, Mrs. Hastings. My dear, *are* you fatigued? Should you prefer that we forgo the theater and let you rest?"

Emmaline pulled free the hand Jeremy had taken hold of as he spoke. "There are no interested eyes to impress here. And I am quite all right!" she said from between clenched teeth. "But as I do not wish to be late, may we be off?"

"Of course, my pet," Jeremy said soothingly, "just as soon as Mrs. Hastings is ready, You would not like to be so rude as to rush her, surely."

At that Mrs. Hastings laughed outright. "Care-ful, my boy, or you may find yourself in the briars."

In mock astonishment Jeremy said, "Nonsense! You cannot mean you think my fiancée has a temper?"

Emmaline closed her eyes and fought for calm. When she opened them, she saw that Mrs. Hastings was ready and the footman was already hold-ing open the door. Solicitously Jeremy said, "Come Emmaline, we must hurry. You said so yourself."

Then, compellingly, he held out a hand to take hers. Emmaline wanted to ignore it, to sail past him with head held high. But she did not. "Very well, I am ready," she said quietly, allowing him to guide her out the door and down the steps.

In the carriage she could not resist challenging him. "Perhaps you ought to ignore me tonight,

Jeremy. Let the *ton* think we are beginning to tire of one another."

A gleam of mischief lit Jeremy's eyes from where he sat opposite her. "But my dear Emmaline, you forget how peaked you look. While I might allow that it would be a good notion to let the *ton* believe we are not suited, I have no wish to figure as an ogre in their eyes. As I surely should if it appeared that I was the cause of your sleepless nights." He paused, then added deliberately, "Am I, my love?"

"Don't be absurd!" Emmaline retorted angrily.

It did not escape him, however, that she caught her lower lip between her teeth as she turned away. With a grim smile of satisfaction he folded his arms across his chest and leaned back against the seat. Emmaline might not yet wish to marry him, but neither was she indifferent.

It was Mrs. Hastings who broke the silence by asking if Emmaline had told Jeremy about her father's latest letter. "But of course not," she answered her own question with a self-conscious laugh. "You have not yet had the chance."

Instantly Jeremy was all attention. "Your father? Is he worse? Do you need to go to him?"

He could not read the expressions that crossed her face so quickly before she said, "Why, no. Quite the opposite, in fact. I—I have not known my father to write a letter in his own hand since before his illness. He had always to dictate it to me or your father. But now he writes and tells me he is much better and I cannot doubt it."

Jeremy had been seated beside Mrs. Hastings and opposite Emmaline, but now he moved to sit beside his fiancée. He took her trembling hand in his and asked gently, "What is it, my love? What is troubling you?"

Emmaline snatched away her hand as though it had been burned and hid it in the folds of her skirt. Her eyes blazing with anger, she said, "Don't roast me, Jeremy! In public you may play the role of attentive lover as much as you choose, but there is no need to do so here."

Biting back the sharp retort that came to his lips, Jeremy merely shrugged and said, "Very well, as you wish. But I should like to know what is troubling you. After all, I do care about your father, too, whatever our own differences may be."

Emmaline did not miss the edge of pain in Jeremy's voice and timidly she placed a hand on his arm. "Forgive me," she said quietly. "I am grateful for the affection you and my father have shared. As for why I am troubled, I—cannot say. I know I should be filled with delight but I am not. Instead I am afraid. Afraid that somehow my father is pushing himself beyond what is wise because I am not there to stop him."

"That is his own choice to make," Jeremy reminded her kindly and, after a moment's hesitation, placed a hand over hers.

This time she did not draw away. Instead, a trifle ruefully she said, "I know it. But I have grown so used, you see, to taking care of him that I can scarcely bring myself to trust anyone else to do the job properly."

The words were spoken lightly but Jeremy did not miss the tremor she could not entirely hide. Tilting up her chin, he asked, "What is it? You

had best tell me, you know, for I shall not give
you any peace until you do."

Emmaline laughed shakily. "I had forgotten how
well you always seemed to read my mind when I
was a child. Very well. You will think me absurd,
no doubt, but *I* know that you mean what you say.
Jeremy, I cannot help but wonder if my father
would have done better had I not been there
these past years. If he can so quickly progress to
writing in his own hand when I am gone scarcely
a month, what might he have done in the past
three years?"

Jeremy did not turn from the steadiness of her
eyes as he replied, "Without you he might well
have died. You know that he loved your mother
very much and I imagine that after she died he
had very little will to live. You gave him a reason
to keep on. I've no doubt of that. And if, in the
past year or two, he had come to accept too easily
his illness and not try harder to recover, well no
one could have foreseen that. Perhaps it is the
knowledge that you are to be wed at last that has
made the difference, and not someone else's care."

"Perhaps," she mused. "My father did write
that he soon hopes to hear marriage vows spoken." Lowering her eyes, she added quietly, "But
I am not, after all, to be wed, am I?"

"Would you like to be, my little termagant?"
Jeremy asked softly, amusement in his voice. "I
thought you had resolved upon spinsterhood?"

"*Spinsterhood?*" Mrs. Hastings was aghast. "Nothing of the sort, my dear! Pray promise me you
have not begun to turn eccentric? Spinsterhood.
You have no notion, Emmaline, what that must
mean to a woman. Either depending upon the

charity of relatives and the necessity to play servant to their needs or, if one is fortunate enough to possess a source of funds, being the butt of gossip about what dire attribute caused that horrid fate. Even at fifty you would find yourself hedged about with conventions you could not bear, for age alone does not release an unmarried woman from the need to play propriety."

Emmaline cast a withering look at Jeremy before turning to placate Mrs. Hastings. "I spoke in anger and well Mr. Barnett knew it. I am neither a feather-wit nor so naive as to believe that the lot of a spinster is an enviable one." Then in a calmer voice she said to Jeremy, "Yes, I should like to be wed. For many reasons, one of which is that I should like to make my father happy. But not at the expense of a lifetime of misery for myself."

Emmaline's eyes challenged him to laugh at her, but Jeremy merely continued to regard her calmly. "May I ask," he said meekly, "what qualities you believe would satisfy you in a man?" Emmaline looked at him suspiciously and would not answer. After a moment he suggested helpfully, "You would like him to be handsome, of course. And possessed of a fortune so that you need not want for anything. He ought to obey your every command and worship the very ground you walk upon. Am I not right?"

"On the contrary, you are quite absurd," she retorted angrily. Swallowing hard, she looked away from him.

Ever persistent, Jeremy once more took her hand in his and said softly, "Very well, then tell me what it is you seek."

Emmaline closed her eyes for a moment, then

turned back to face him, tilting up her chin. "I should like to marry a man who cares about the same things I do. Someone who will share the troubled times with me as well as the good. And I wish to marry someone I love. But that is something you could not understand, I am sure."

"Love?" There was a note of triumph to Jeremy's voice. One Emmaline had not heard before as he went on smoothly, "And you fancy yourself in love with someone, do you?"

Panic seized Emmaline. Mrs. Hastings leaped to her rescue. In a derisive voice she told Jeremy, "You need not be thinking, Barnett, that she means you. I've no doubt there are any number of far more eligible, far more obliging gentlemen in London than you."

Jeremy regarded Emmaline warily and she hastily looked away. Instinct told her not to lie to him and yet she could not bring herself to contradict Mrs. Hastings. Perhaps that lady did indeed know what was best, and in any event, Emmaline found she had no wish for her deepest feelings to be bared to Jeremy when he was in a mood such as this. "You've fallen in love with someone here in London?" he demanded harshly. Emmaline nodded, not trusting herself to speak. "And does he love you?" Jeremy persisted coolly.

"I—I have no reason to think so," she whispered in reply.

"And yet you still wish to marry him?" Jeremy demanded mockingly. "Are you sure your love is not simply an illusion?"

"If it is, then it is a remarkably sound illusion," Emmaline retorted tartly.

Jeremy shrugged irritably. "A fortune hunter,

no doubt. And I suppose you would marry him if he asked, even knowing he does not love you? I tell you frankly, you are a fool if you do. I have seen too many such marriages to believe they can ever work."

Anger had straightened her spine and Emmaline no longer doubted the wisdom of her course. It was with a grim smile that she replied, "So too have I, and it is the one reason I am not yet at the altar."

"Is it?" Jeremy laughed harshly. "You forget, there is another. We are still officially betrothed, my love, and you would need my agreement to send a notice to the papers breaking it off. And I tell you now I will not do so in order for you to marry some fellow I do not know. My sense of responsibility toward you is far too great to allow it."

Grimly Emmaline replied, "You already know him."

The same thought occurred to both Mrs. Hastings and Jeremy. Their eyes meeting by accident, the two hastily looked away. Mrs. Hastings had forgotten that she herself had started the falsehood. Instead it was the thought of her son that leaped to mind. This time it was Jeremy who carefully looked toward the window of the carriage. "I see," he said roughly. "It seems you still have the power to surprise me, Emmaline. I had not thought love grew so quickly."

"I have heard it said that love can spring up, full blown, in a moment," her voice replied steadily.

"And if he marries someone else?" Jeremy asked.

"Then I suppose I shall nurse a broken heart."

"Even if he is not worth it?" Jeremy demanded roughly.

He had turned to face her again and Emmaline met his eyes steadily. "Who is to say whether or not he is worth it?"

She might have added more had Mrs. Hastings' voice not then intruded. "Children," she said with some asperity, "we have arrived. And unless you wish to make us conspicuous by your conversation, I suggest you put the matter aside until another time."

The coachman opened the door as Mrs. Hastings spoke, and they were soon all inside the theater. In spite of Emmaline's fears, they were not late but neither were they so early that they could afford to dawdle on the way to the Hastings box.

"I do hope Edward and Miss Kirkwood and her mother have already arrived," Mrs. Hastings said, fanning herself furiously.

Something must be done about her son and Miss Delwyn, she vowed, but at the moment she could not see just what.

15

EDWARD arrived at the Kirkwood household to discover everyone in something of a dither. Lady Kirkwood had found herself indisposed just as she was to have dressed to accompany her daughter to the theater. Now it was out of the question that either of them should go. If Rosalind had been her usual dutiful self, there would have been no problem. Mr. Hastings would have arrived and been given the regrets of the Kirkwood ladies and gone on to the theater by himself. When Rosalind was informed of this scenario, however, she had shown herself to be astonishingly willful.

"I *am* going to the theater with Mr. Hastings and Emmaline and Mr. Barnett, Mama," she said quietly but firmly.

"You cannot," her mother replied icily. "Nor, I assure you, would Mr. Hastings or the others expect you to."

"Oh, but I shall," Rosalind persisted. "I have promised Emmaline. She will be there, so you need have no fear as to the proprieties."

As Lady Kirkwood was immediately ill into the washbasin held by a maidservant, it was some moments before she could form an answer to this evidence of rebellion. Moreover, she had not yet changed out of her day dress and did not dare to try. Indeed, as it was, there were times when the bed seemed to her to be moving most disastrously. Lady Kirkwood was therefore a trifle ill-tempered when she was finally able to reply, "That is not in the least sufficient and well you know it! Besides, the Marquess of Alnwick will be returning to London tomorrow for the celebrations and will expect to see you. I've no wish for him to hear I have been careless of your reputation. You'll stay home with me."

Rosalind took a deep breath. "No, Mama. I am going to the theater with or without your permission."

"Fine talking, my girl," Lady Kirkwood said severely. "But do you really think Mr. Hastings will take you if he knows it is against my wishes?"

To her mother's astonishment, Rosalind smiled. "No, of course he would not. He is far too much of a gentleman." She paused for effect before she went on, "If you do not allow me to go with Mr. Hastings, then I shall wait until he is gone and slip out—as you well know I am capable of doing—and hire a hackney to take me to the theater, where Mr. Hastings and Mr. Barnett and even Emmaline will no doubt conclude that I must be brought home straightaway. But by then I will no doubt have become the focus of a great many eyes, perhaps even more than the performers on stage, and I shall become the subject of the latest *on-dit*."

She paused and then added gently, "I don't think you would like that very much, Mama. Particularly if you are so afraid of what the Marquess of Alnwick will say. Indeed, I am almost persuaded I ought to do something of the sort anyway."

Lady Kirkwood was again too sick to answer right away. A good many thoughts ran through her head, however, including the recollection that his lordship's first words upon seeing his newborn daughter had been that the baby was rather ugly and a trifle under the limit and perhaps they ought to throw it back. Just now Lady Kirkwood was inclined to wish they had done so.

Nothing had been resolved, although Lady Kirkwood was feeling over the worst of her illness, when Mr. Hastings was announced. "I shall not," she said, fixing her daughter with an exasperated stare, "allow you to tell him the situation yourself. Nor will I forget, I promise you, that you dragged me from my sickbed with your nonsensical stubbornness!"

Rosalind merely continued to regard her mother tranquilly and even with an unseemly amount of interest. Together they went downstairs.

"My dear Mr. Hastings," Lady Kirkwood greeted him nervously, "you find us in disarray tonight, I fear. I am unable to go to the theater and don't quite know how to tell Rosalind she may not either. You and Mr. Barnett have always behaved with perfect propriety toward us, and Emmaline will be there but—"

She broke off in confusion and Edward finished for her, smiling wryly, "But he and I, particularly Jeremy, have such wretched reputations." She nodded with relief and Edward said thoughtfully, "I do understand, of course, and can only regret that our past pranks now stand in the way of Miss

Kirkwood's enjoyment of the theater tonight. But perhaps you did not understand that my mother will be there as well? And that she will undertake to bring Miss Kirkwood home herself?"

Lady Kirkwood sighed. A trifle tremulously she said, "Yes. That would make a difference, of course. Yes, I do think I could let her go then. And now, pray excuse me, I am about to be indisposed again."

This last was spoken with rather unseemly haste and Lady Kirkwood fled before Edward had time even to express his pleasure that she had relented concerning Rosalind. Turning to the girl, he said softly, "Perhaps we should leave before your mother has time to change her mind?"

"Yes, let us go at once," Rosalind agreed hastily. "How fortunate that Mama became indisposed *after* I had already dressed and not before."

After he had handed her into the carriage a few moments later, given his coachman the necessary instructions, and shut the carriage door behind them, Edward said gravely, "You are more beautiful than ever tonight, Miss Kirkwood."

"And you are so handsome," Rosalind replied breathlessly, "though I suppose I ought not to say that. Mama is forever telling me to guard my tongue or I shall give gentlemen a distaste of me."

Sitting beside her and gently taking Rosalind's hand, Edward smiled down at her. "I assure you, I don't mind," he said. "And she is not here to know that you said it."

For a long moment they stared at one another, then Rosalind abruptly pulled free her hand. "We—we must not," she said.

"Why not?" he asked, then blushed as she did.

Together they said, "Jeremy."

"Do you feel a *tendre* for him?" Edward asked hesitantly. "Would you be distressed if he married Miss Delwyn after all?"

Still blushing, Rosalind shook her head. "No, I should like it above all things."

A trifle surprised, Edward said cautiously, "Yet you do not appear to have discouraged his attentions."

"But that was only because Emmaline—" Rosalind broke off in confusion. Fighting to regain her composure, she said, "You appear to have been championing Jeremy's cause with me. Have you come not to wish it?"

"I never—" he began.

"Then why—?" they said together.

In dismay they stared at one another until a smile began to tug at the corners of their mouths. "I think," Edward said judiciously, "that we had best compare notes."

"All right," she said shyly. Then, taking a deep breath, she said, "Emmaline thought that it would be safer for Jeremy to have his eye on me than some other girl who might marry him." She paused and giggled. "I was to drive him crazy by being outrageous in my demands and such."

"Which is why you told him you must have that certain flavor of ice that Gunther's was out of so that he was forced to bribe them to procure it," Edward hazarded with a reminiscent smile. "Which Jeremy did only to outrage Emmaline and make her jealous that he would go to such lengths for you yesterday! What a pity he never even saw her and so the gesture went to waste."

Rosalind looked at Edward, puzzlement evident upon her face. "But why would he wish to make her jealous?" she asked slowly. "Unless he is in love with her—but that's impossible because if he was there wouldn't be any reason they shouldn't marry and they would and Jeremy wouldn't get upset every time he is asked their wedding date."

Edward regarded her quizzically. "At first he was terrified of marriage and angry that his father forced him to the step. But it has been some time," he said gently, "since Jeremy stopped being afraid. It is Emmaline who refuses to marry him or to believe that his sentiments have undergone a change."

"What are we going to do about it?" Rosalind asked.

"That is precisely what I am asking myself," he replied. "I know it shan't be as simple as telling them what we know. Two more stubborn people I have never met."

With a shiver Rosalind replied, "Too right you are! When once Emmaline takes on a notion it is almost impossible to shake her from it."

"Jeremy as well," Edward said grimly. Then, more gently, "Let me think about it. We'll talk again tomorrow and perhaps by then I'll have some notions."

At his words, Rosalind remembered that the Marquess of Alnwick was due back then and she could not help but shiver. Something of her distress conveyed itself to Edward, who immediately asked, "What is it, Rosalind? What is wrong?"

Looking down at her hands, she said so softly he could scarcely hear her, "We shall not be able to talk after tomorrow, I fear."

"Why not?" Edward demanded in confusion.

Rosalind raised her eyes to his and could not

hide the plea in hers. "You must know my parents wish me to marry a certain . . . certain gentleman. He returns to London tomorrow to claim me. I shall not marry him, of course, but I've no doubt my parents will be so angry they shall bundle me off home or some such thing and forbid me to see any of my friends."

"They would not dare," Edward told her steadily. "Tomorrow I'll speak to your father and I assure you that after I have, he will not dare to so mistreat you." He paused and then said hesitantly, "That is, if you will trust me and give me the right to speak to him for you."

Shyly Rosalind tucked a hand in his. "I shall trust you always," she said very simply.

He looked down at her and said, "You shall never regret it, I swear." Then, as the carriage jolted to a halt he added, "We're here. No doubt Jeremy and Emmaline and my mother have already arrived."

He was right, of course. Lady Kirkwood's hesitation had taken longer than any of them realized and it was only as the curtain was rising that they took their seats in the box, Rosalind beside Jeremy and Edward beside Emmaline with Mrs. Hastings to the rear.

"But my dear, where is your mother?" Mrs. Hastings asked Rosalind.

The girl blushed prettily as she said, "My mother was indisposed and could not come but knew that you would be here and said I need not stay home with her."

"I assured her that you would take Rosalind home yourself," Edward told his mother.

"Well, of course I shall, " she said, a trifle affronted. "However, I am very glad you could come, my dear. Perhaps you would rather change places with Emmaline? The view is, I believe, a bit better."

Emmaline and Jeremy could not help but over-hear these words and Emmaline colored as Jeremy regarded Mrs. Hastings with raised eyebrows. Neither, however, made a protest as the chairs were rearranged. Emmaline could only be grate-ful that the play had already begun so that most eyes were turned upon the stage and few free to watch their box. She had no desire to have curious tongues speculate on the change.

So rapt was her own attention to the tale on stage that it came as something of a surprise when the curtain was rung down for intermission. At once, Jeremy and Edward were on their feet. "May we procure you some refreshments?" they asked the ladies.

"Or perhaps you would care to walk with us?" Jeremy asked, a trifle stiffly.

Not trusting herself to speak, Emmaline merely shook her head. After their words in the carriage, the last thing she wished was to be by his side, walking with him, subject to whatever tongue lash-ing he chose to give her this time. Rosalind an-swered for them, saying, "We'll stay here. I—I feel a trifle faint." At once everyone was all sympathy and, coloring, Rosalind waved away their concern. "I shall be quite all right," she assured them, "it is just the heat tonight. Pray go and fetch us some lemonade."

When they were gone, Mrs. Hastings turned her attention to the other boxes and Rosalind and Emmaline were left to themselves. Rosalind was about to speak to her friend when abruptly the door to their box opened and all three women turned to see a gentleman and lady standing in the doorway. He was elegantly dressed if in a somewhat old-fashioned way and leaned slightly upon a silver-headed cane. The lady wore a green silk gown that exactly matched her eyes.

It was on the tip of Mrs. Hastings' tongue to ask if they had mistaken their box when suddenly Emmaline was on her feet and throwing her arms around the man. "Papa!" she cried. "Mrs. Colton. Whatever are you doing in London?"

Sir Osbert gently disentangled his daughter's arms from about his neck and said with a smile, "Why, come to see you, of course. But pray, curtsy to your new stepmother. She is Mrs. Colton no longer."

In bewilderment Emmaline turned to the lady, who also smiled and said gently, "I hope you will not be distressed, my dear, that your father and I were married yesterday. He would not write and tell you but insisted it was better to come and surprise you himself." She paused and her eyes danced as she added, "Your father can be a most persuasive man when he chooses."

"But his health," Emmaline protested. "Did the doctor say it was all right?"

"The doctor is a fool, but he allowed that I am in better health than I have been since before your mother died," Sir Osbert told his daughter roundly. Drawing his wife's arm through his, he said, patting her hand affectionately, "It seems I needed someone like Anna to bring me back to myself."

"Do you forgive us for shocking you like this?" Anna asked Emmaline.

"Forgive us? Nonsense!" Sir Osbert retorted. "She would never be so undaughterly as to say so even if she thought she had the right to an opinion on the matter. Which she does not," he concluded, fixing his daughter with a pointed stare.

Emmaline blinked rapidly, her voice a trifle tremulous as she replied, "Forgive you? I am so happy for you!"

Impulsively she hugged her new stepmother and drew her forward into the box. "Mrs. Hastings, Rosalind, I should like you to meet my father and his wife."

They greeted Rosalind, who curtsied very prettily. Then Mrs. Hastings kissed Sir Osbert and his new wife. "I am so pleased for you," she said frankly. "And delighted you came to London to see us. How long do you remain, Lady Delwyn? Where are you staying?"

"At the Clarendon," Sir Osbert replied. Then, with a twinkle in his eyes, he said, "We came to see the celebrations in the parks, tomorrow. The papers have been full of the preparations and we promised ourselves we would not miss them for the world. And of course we mean to see Emmaline wed. My dear, your letters telling us how happy you are made us impatient to see you tie the knot yourself."

In dismay, Emmaline could only stare at her father. All at once the letters she had sent, meant to reassure him when he was so ill, seemed a grave mistake. Rosalind, usually so meek, sprang to her aid. In a voice that was a trifle breathless she said saucily, "There is someone else who needs to be consulted before the plans are made surely? Mr. Barnett."

"Yes, we expect him back to the box any moment," Mrs. Hastings said tranquilly.

Sir Osbert waved a careless hand. "Oh, he may be a little delayed. His father is here in London with us. He wishes to see the Chinese pagoda, you know. But right now I've no doubt he and Jeremy are in conversation and have much to say to one another." He hesitated; then, looking pale, he said quietly, "I pray you will forgive me if I sit down. I am much better but still need to have a care for my health."

Immediately everyone hastened to make him comfortable. When he was settled, his wife, who was still standing, said with a fond smile, "Don't worry. We shall have him right as a trivet in no time."

Just then the door of the box once more opened and Edward and Jeremy and Lord Barnett were standing there with everyone looking as pale as Sir Osbert.

16

SOMEHOW they got through the rest of the evening. Fortunately the curtain had gone up immediately, and by the time the play had ended both Jeremy and Emmaline had regained control of their voices. With creditable calm they had bid their fathers good night. Jeremy had even managed to commandeer Edward's carriage, saying, "You and your mother will wish to take Rosalind home. And Emmaline and I have much to speak about. Certain, er, plans to make."

"Yes, of course you do," Sir Osbert said approvingly. "But mind you take my daughter straight round to Mrs. Hastings' house and speak further there with her if you must. After all, you are not yet wed, you know, and I've no mind to have my daughter provide speaking matter for all the tattleboxes of London."

Jeremy nodded curtly and hastened Emmaline out of there as quickly as possible. Nor could he keep from cursing at the delay as they waited for Edward's carriage to reach the door. The coachman, fortunately, accepted his hasty explanation of the change of plans without a quibble. Aside from being well trained, he was used to seeing

Jeremy with his master and accustomed, by now, to their eccentricities.

As the carriage pulled away from the theater Jeremy rounded on Emmaline and demanded, "What the devil prompted your father to come to London? And just what have you been writing in your letters that makes him want an immediate wedding?"

Emmaline shrank back against the squabs, "Only what we agreed upon. That our betrothal was going well. That I was happy. That I missed him and hoped Mrs. Colton was taking good care of him."

"You must have said something more," he persisted.

"Why?" she demanded. "Why must it be something I have written? Why not something you did or said to *your* father? He is here as well, after all."

"Perhaps," Jeremy conceded with poor grace. "In any event it scarcely matters. They are here now and expecting that damnable wedding and if we are not careful we shall find ourselves leg-shackled against our wishes. That will put paid to your chances with the man you love, and I . . . I have no taste for such a marriage."

"So you have made very clear to me," Emmaline retorted bitterly.

"Emmaline, had things been different, had you not fallen in love with this other man, could you have married me?" Jeremy asked hesitantly.

She looked at him a long time before answering. "Married a man who shrank from the notion? You need not pretend otherwise for I would not believe you. No, I cannot imagine such a marriage except as a sort of impossible hell."

As she spoke, Jeremy turned his face away from her. "I see," he said at last. "I have no taste, either, for marriage to someone who shrinks from such a step."

"What shall we do, then?" Emmaline asked quietly, praying he would not read from her face the ache his words had aroused in her breast.

He did not answer right away. For one mad moment Jeremy considered marrying Emmaline and be damned with scruples! Be damned with this other fellow she believed herself in love with! But, closing his eyes, Jeremy knew he could not do it. Not when the example of his own uncle was so clearly before him. That fellow had married the woman he loved, over her objections, and she had come to hate him. A bitter, angry woman, she led him the devil's own dance until finally she ran away with a man she claimed she did love and he shut himself away in the countryside, unable to face the scandal or the condolences of his friends.

When the words finally came, there was a dull bitterness to Jeremy's voice that could not escape Emmaline. "You need do nothing. I shall take great care that I am the villain of the piece and everyone will feel sorry for you and congratulate you upon your fortunate escape."

"But what do you mean to do?" Emmaline persisted.

Slowly he turned to face her. "I shall marry Miss Kirkwood. It will not be an ideal match but at least she will not have to marry the Marquess of Alnwick. Edward tells me he returns to London tomorrow and she is very much afraid of him, for which no one can blame her. Anyway, I shall contrive to speak with her and arrange for us to run away together tomorrow night. Then you need never see me again, if that is your wish."

A trifle shakily Emmaline said, "You forget, she is my best friend."

Bitterness still tinged Jeremy's voice as he replied, "You need have no fear. I shall take care always to be away when you come to call. You need not fear I shall embarrass you. Then, after a time, you can wed the man you love."

Looking down at her hands, Emmaline said hollowly, "That will not be possible."

Roughly he said to her, "You think that now, but I tell you it will all work out." He paused, then said in a voice heavy with sarcasm, "Have you an alternate plan?"

"Tell our fathers the truth?" she offered hesitantly.

Jeremy turned away. "You know what my father will say. And your own, in spite of how well he looked tonight, might not stand the shock."

"And you think he will stand the shock of discovering you have eloped with another woman better?" Emmaline demanded roundly.

"He will when you explain that you have mistaken your feelings for me and fallen in love with another man," Jeremy said inexorably. "Then he will only be grateful for your narrow escape from marriage to me."

Despair washed over Emmaline. If ever there had been a chance to straighten out matters between herself and Jeremy, it was rapidly slipping away. Nor did it help when he took her hand gently and said with quiet sincerity, "I had not meant to hurt you, my dear. Will you remember me with at least a little affection?"

"A little?" she cried, snatching her hand away.

Jeremy leaned back against the squabs. His voice was cold as he said, "Forgive me. I had not realized your distaste ran so deep. There was a time when I thought you looked upon me with more than kindness. Evidently I have managed to destroy even that in you. My apologies. I can only repeat that I shall never distress you again." Emmaline started to speak and he held up a hand. "No. Don't say anything more. There is no point. We will soon be at the Hastings town house. I am sure you will forgive me if I do not escort you in."

And that was that. Looking at Jeremy's implacable profile, Emmaline could not bring herself to speak. Instead she sat miserably in her corner of the carriage, waves of despair continuing to wash over her. Had he seen the way she fled to her room upon reaching the Hastings household, and cried herself to sleep, he would certainly have altered his plans.

As it was, Jeremy returned to his own bachelor rooms, there to await Edward, who he knew would come. By the time Hastings arrived Jeremy was already well into a bottle of port. Tossing his hat and gloves on a nearby table, Edward drew up a chair next to Jeremy and said, "Well, my friend, what do you do now?"

Jeremy laughed harshly. "Why, I get married, of course," he said simply.

Edward blinked, then grinned and clapped his friend on the shoulder. "I'm very happy for you! I presume then that you and Emmaline have reconciled and all is well?"

Irritably Jeremy shook free the hand. "We have done nothing of the sort," he said roughly. "She is in love with someone else. You, in fact; or so I suspect. And I hope you will be happy together." At his friend's start of surprise Jeremy added, "You have more than once told me that if Emmaline were your fiancée, your eyes would not wander elsewhere. Well, here is your chance. If you are not in love with her yet, you soon will be when I am out of the way."

A frown upon his face, Edward leaned back in his chair. In a voice that was carefully neutral he said, "Did Emmaline tell you she has a *tendre* for me?"

"She said she was in love and that it is someone I know, someone who is here in London and who is not yet in love with her. Who else could it be? I have seen how much at ease she is in your company, Edward, which she is not, for all her social success, with anyone else."

For a long moment Hastings regarded his friend, choosing the words he would say. At last he suggested quietly, "Perhaps she means you, Jeremy."

Barnett laughed harshly. "She has made it very plain she does not. She has even made it clear that she should prefer spinsterhood to being leg-shackled to me. I have lost her, destroyed whatever chance we might have had together." There was genuine anguish in his eyes as he said, "I am not accustomed to this, Edward. Never did I think the day would come when a woman would run from me and not I from her."

"I see. Your damnable pride is hurt," Hastings suggested derisively.

"Damn you, it is far more than that!" Jeremy cursed his friend. "I've fallen in love with her. Too much in love to chain her to me for life."

"You were willing to do so a few days ago," Edward pointed out.

"That was before I knew how mistaken I was concerning her feelings toward me," Jeremy curtly.

"Perhaps you were right then and mistaken now," Edward suggested mildly.

Jeremy regarded Hastings steadily as he said, "You have encouraged me in this folly all along. Because of your fondness for both of us, you wished to believe Emmaline and I could be wed. I no longer trust your judgment on the matter, my friend."

"But—" Hastings began.

"No!" Jeremy all but shouted the word.

Edward shrugged. "Very well, what do you mean to do?" he asked reasonably, his eyes hooded.

Jeremy got to his feet and began to pace the room. "I? I shall marry. Someone else. Then neither my father nor hers can blame Emmaline or force her into marriage to me when she so evidently does not wish it."

"And whom do you mean to marry?" Edward asked warily.

"Rosalind" was the prompt reply. At his friend's second start of surprise Jeremy went on, a trifle impatiently, "Why not? You have said yourself that the Marquess of Alnwick returns to London tomorrow. The girl would do anything to escape the fate of being wed to him and I flatter myself that she, at least, does not hold me in dislike. It will not be an ideal marriage but better than the torture of being wed to a woman who will hate me for it." He did not wait for a reply nor look at Edward to see the distress upon his friend's face. Instead he pressed on, "I shall need your help, of course, Edward. You must be the go-between, both for Rosalind and Emmaline. She must be forewarned so that she is prepared to explain matters to her father. Will you do it, my friend?"

For what seemed an interminable time to Jeremy, the silence stretched on. At last, with a curious half smile upon his face, Edward said, "Why yes, Jeremy, I shall. You may leave everything in my hands. I shall arrange whatever horses and carriage may be needed and arrange everything with Rosalind and even warn Emmaline. I presume you mean to flee to Gretna Green?"

"Of course. Mind you, now," Jeremy said seriously, "Miss Kirkwood's mother must not get wind of the affair. She would do her utmost to stop us."

"You may trust me implicitly," Edward replied.

It was Jeremy's turn to clap his friend upon the shoulder. Then, once more pacing the room, he began to speak aloud his thoughts. "Not too early and yet not so late that her disappearance will at once be remarked upon. I have it! Everyone in London will be at the celebrations tomorrow night. It will be a terrific crush and nothing could be simpler than to slip away. Rosalind will not at once be missed, and even when she is, it will be some time before an alarm is sounded. It will merely be assumed that she and I were separated from the others in the crowd. And I know she will be there for she has been for some time pledged to accompany Emmaline."

"So she has," Edward agreed gravely. "And you are quite right that there will be much confusion. Anything might be laid to that particular door." A smile played about his lips before he concluded,

"Yes, tomorrow night should be quite a night before we are through."

There was another silence and then Edward said carelessly, "I still say it is a pity you and Emmaline could not have made it up between you. But no doubt you will soon forget that you ever might have wed her."

With a bleakness that even took Edward aback Jeremy replied, "I shall never forget. No, nor cease regretting that by my recklessness I lost the one chance I might have had at true happiness. Oh, don't mistake me. I mean to be a good husband to Rosalind. I shall owe her that much. And I think we shall even rub along tolerably well together. But with Emmaline—with Emmaline I might have shared something much more."

"And yet you would see her married to me?" Edward asked with eyebrows raised in disbelief.

Jeremy flung himself to the far corner of the room. "No, damn you, I would not see her married to anyone other than myself. And I tell you now that if you marry her I will never come to your house to see you together. But neither do I wish upon her spinsterhood. If it is marriage with you she wishes, then that is far better. I only ask that if you do come to wed her that you do so when I am far from London. Perhaps I shall take Rosalind to the Continent after we are married and you will have time to court Emmaline." He paused and anger gave way to the same bleakness as before. "You need only send me a line when the deed is done," he said, "and it is safe for me to come back to England."

"Will that be any easier?" Edward asked mildly.

"Once you are wed I shall have no choice but to

accept it," Jeremy replied roughly. "But I would not trust myself not to stop the wedding if I were nearby when it took place. Now go. I mean to drink myself into oblivion and I find I can no longer bear to look at your face."

To his annoyance, Edward did not rise but instead said mildly, "I'm afraid you are out of luck my friend, for I mean to stay." At Jeremy's look of outrage he added innocently, "We have, after all, a great many details to work out, you know. I should prefer to be able to set out tomorrow and take care of everything without constantly having to return here to consult with you."

"You are right, of course, damn you," Jeremy said. "Stay, then, if you must, but drink along with me. Have a glass of port and toast my forthcoming marriage."

"Do you know, I think I shall," was the calm reply.

17

EMMALINE found it difficult to face her father the next morning. Only the habit of hiding from Sir Osbert the fears she had for his health now allowed her to greet him with any semblance of equanimity. To her critical eyes his color seemed even better than yesterday as he sank into a sofa with crocodile legs. Relief and pleasure at having him so restored to health caused her to say breathlessly, "How wonderful to have you here, Papa! But where is Mrs.—Anna?"

Sir Osbert regarded his daughter with a wry smile. "She thought we might like to see one another alone," he said kindly. "That we might feel freer to talk if she were not about. Tell me, Emmaline, are you truly not distressed over the marriage? Mind, I'll tell you frankly that I have no regrets and will not even if you tell me you hate her. But I should like to know how you feel."

"Oh Papa," she chided him playfully, "as if I could be other than happy if you are. And if you are wondering if I am recollecting Mama, I can only say that I believe she would be happy for you as well. No, I have always been fond of Anna. The only thing I do not understand is why you did not tell me beforehand."

Sir Osbert held out a hand and drew his daughter onto the sofa beside him. "I wanted it to be a surprise," he said. "I was afraid that if you knew our plans you would feel you must come home to be there. And if you came, you would have seen how much better I was and I didn't want you to until we were certain that my recovery was permanent. Can you understand?"

"Of course, Papa."

"Good. Now tell me what plans you and Jeremy have hatched for your own wedding," he said with a smile.

Emmaline could not meet her father's eyes. Stammering a trifle, she said, "I—I cannot, today. After all you must allow us some surprises of our own, Papa. But I promise you that tomorrow I shall tell you everything."

He chuckled. "Very well. Under the circumstances I can scarcely fault you for that. Just so long as you promise me you will not marry without having me present. I intend to throw you a wonderful wedding and you are not to cheat me of that pleasure."

With perfect honesty and an ache that did not betray itself in her well schooled features Emmaline said, "I promise you, Father, I shall not be married without you there."

There was a moment of warm silence before Emmaline said hastily, "How are Adeline and Caroline? What did they think of your marriage?"

Sir Osbert's lips pressed together in a thin line of anger. "They were not pleased. Adeline could not forget that the year is scarcely up since Mr. Colton's death. Caroline was little better. But they cannot know as I do what Anna was forced to endure as the wife of that man. I have pledged to myself that I will erase the unhappiness of those memories for her."

"But she never gave us any notion she was not content," Emmaline said slowly. "I never heard he was other than an exemplary husband."

"Anna was not a woman to confide her troubles or press them on others. Nor were his lapses the sort that would have been told to a young girl such as yourself, Emmaline," he said grimly. Then, taking hold of his daughter's hands, he said, "Did you never wonder that even when the fashions were for short sleeves Anna always wore hers long? Or why so often she was indisposed for days at a time and would see no one?"

Sir Osbert paused and regarded his daughter shrewdly. "You need not think," he went on, "that even now she has told me all this. I found it out for myself some years ago from Colton. He was fool enough to brag to me once when he was in his cups that he knew how to keep a wife in line and that there was even a certain pleasure in beating her. I told him that if I ever discovered he had done so again, I would call him out and damn the consequences. So far as I know, he did not so long as I was well. What happened after I became ill I have not yet been able to discover. I cannot bring myself, you see, to press Anna to speak of matters that must be painful to her."

"Oh Papa, I never knew," Emmaline said, all her sympathies aroused.

Sir Osbert patted her hand, "Well, now you

know why I am so determined to watch out for your happiness. Why with your sisters I refused certain suitors, even some far more eligible than those they married. I do not say their marriages are perfect, but that is one horror they will never know. Nor you. For all his faults, a pleasure in beating women cannot be laid at Jeremy's door. Indeed, I think marriage to you will be the making of him, for at bottom I believe he is a good man."

"So do I," Emmaline said huskily.

"Good. Well, enough of that. I have promised I shall not press you until tomorrow as to the date and such and I will not. Let us talk instead of the festivities. When I arose this morning, I was very much afraid it would rain all day, but now I begin to think the weather may clear after all. Do you go to Green Park to see Sadler's balloon ascent or to the Serpentine to view the regatta? And tonight, do you favor the Chinese pagoda at St. James Park or the fair at Hyde Park or the Gothic castle at Green Park?"

Emmaline could not help but laugh at her father's eagerness. "I fear we are already too late to see the balloon ascent. All the best places will have been taken. In any event I must wait for Rosalind to arrive and then Edward and Jeremy are to escort us we know not where. They have told us the entire day is to be full of surprises. We didn't know, you see, that you would be in town. Perhaps we could change those plans."

"No, no. Don't change a thing. Your plans sound delightful," her father said. "And you are not to worry about me. I shall be off to collect Anna and

drive round to the Serpentine. They are to reen-
act the Battle of the Nile, you know, and I wouldn't
miss it for the world. If we do not see one another
during the day, I shall come round tonight or in
the morning and we may compare notes."

Emmaline laughed. "I know what it is," she
teased, "you have taken my desertion so well because you are here in London on your honeymoon and don't want any others hanging about to
interfere. Not even your dearest daughter."

"Quite right," her father told her with a twinkle
in his eyes. "I mean to enjoy myself at last."

Emmaline saw her father to the door and then
returned to the drawing room, where she could
not help but wonder where everyone was. Mr.
Hastings had gone out of London on some estate
business. He had told them all frankly that the
hurly-burly of the first of August was just the sort
of thing he disliked most.

Mrs. Hastings had gone out early, telling Emmaline that for once they would have to dispense
with a chaperon and that while it was a pity, no
one would be likely to notice or care on a day like
today. She would be back in the evening. But
Emmaline had not yet seen Edward. As for Rosalind and Jeremy, they were unaccountably late as
well. Emmaline found herself unabashedly hoping
that Rosalind or Jeremy would be unable or unwilling to carry through on the plan Jeremy had
confided to her the night before. In their absence
she could not help but fear that they had already
flown for the border. It was scarcely surprising,
then, that even the new flowered muslin dress she
wore could not raise her spirits.

A carriage pulled up in front of the Hastings town house, and Emmaline watched from the window with intense relief as Edward handed Rosalind out of the carriage. That feeling changed to irritation, however, as they laughed together and Emmaline realized that both were evidently delighted with the day and seemed not to have a care in the world. Surely they must know by now Jeremy's plan. Didn't it cause them even a little concern? And where, for that matter, was Jeremy?

If she had expected explanations, however, Emmaline was much mistaken. Edward's first words to her were, "Come along! We're late. If we hurry, we may just be in time to see the balloon ascent from a distance."

"Where is Jeremy?" she could not help but ask, drawing back a trifle.

The other two exchanged a look and then began to laugh. Edward recovered first. "Oh, Jeremy isn't coming," he said carelessly. "He was three sheets to the wind last night and I doubt he'll wake before noon. But that's no reason for us to miss the fun!"

As she looked at her friend, Emmaline could not help but realize that Rosalind looked happier than she had ever known her to be. "I—I think I've forgotten something," she stammered. "Come upstairs with me, Rosalind?"

"Here, here, we've no time for that," Edward said with mock severity. "We must be off at once. Whatever you've forgotten can't be that important."

"Quite right," Rosalind seconded him at once.

Emmaline allowed herself to be drawn out to the carriage. As Edward handed her in she asked quietly, "Did Jeremy speak with you about his plans?"

"Yes, yes," he said impatiently, "and I have spoken with Rosalind and arranged everything. But we have hours before we need talk about that."

Swallowing, Emmaline settled into the seat. So her dearest friend did mean to marry Jeremy after all and even looked forward to the event. Neither of Emmaline's companions appeared to take the slightest notice of her megrims and instead kept up a steady chatter of nonsense as the coachman forced his way through the crowded streets. True to his word, Edward had them there in time to see the ropes cut and the balloon rise. He even was able to regale them with all sorts of bits of information as to the history of such ascents and how they were accomplished.

From there he whisked them off to the Serpentine. Once again they were too late to acquire any of the better vantage points; nevertheless, they could see some of the races. Before the mock battle started, however, Edward whisked them off homeward, saying, "Must give you ladies time to rest a bit, then change." He paused, then added significantly, "And make whatever preparations are necessary. You needn't pack anything, Rosalind. I shall take care of whatever you need and leave it at Jeremy's for tonight."

They left Rosalind off at her house first then drove home. Edward seemed unfeelingly cheerful and finally Emmaline said seriously, "It is tonight, I suppose? Jeremy's elopement with Rosalind?"

"Shh," Edward told her with a flourish of his hand, "one wouldn't want the coachman to overhear. As for tonight, well, let me simply say that I expect everything to be settled by morning."

"Morning!" Emmaline exclaimed. "Surely they cannot reach Gretna Green by then?"

"Nevertheless, matters will be settled by morning," Edward assured her. "But we shall require your help."

"Mine?" Emmaline asked faintly.

"Why yes," Edward said innocently. "We do not wish to attract attention and I thought it best that you accompany Rosalind to the posting inn. And wait there until she is off. I know she will feel better for it, if you do. Surely we can count on you for that much?"

"Oh, surely," Emmaline replied in the same faint voice.

"Good!" Edward said. "I knew you were a right one."

They had reached the Hastings household and Edward escorted her inside after instructing the coachman to wait for him. Once inside he made sure the drawing room was deserted before he explained.

"Now then, here is the plan. We shall slip away during the fireworks. You and Rosalind and I will take one hackney to the inn and Jeremy another. Just to confuse anyone who might chance to see us. He will meet us there, at the Cat and Hound. We may be a trifle late returning home tonight, but so will everyone else. I daresay no one will notice, and even if they do, they will put it down to the celebrations and the crowded streets. Tomorrow we can explain everything to everyone."

"Tomorrow," Emmaline echoed. "Edward, I don't

think I can. Face everyone tomorrow, I mean. Particularly your mother. After we have sent Jeremy and Rosalind off, would you take me round to the Clarendon to stay with my father and his wife? I've no doubt they will wish me at Jericho for intruding at such a time, but they may send me back to Selborne straightaway tomorrow."

"Oh, whatever you wish, once matters are settled," Edward said handsomely. "Well, I must be off. Things to do before this evening, you know."

And why his kindly agreement and cheerfulness should lower her spirits even further was beyond understanding, Emmaline told herself roundly. At which point she promptly burst into tears.

18

WHEN Edward Hastings reached Jeremy's quarters, he found his friend in a distinctly ill temper. Edward could not entirely suppress a smile as he asked sympathetically, "Is something the matter, Jeremy?"

Barnett flung a curse at his friend and added, "You know very well I've the devil of a head today. There must have been something wrong with the wine."

"Not the wine, the quantity of it that you drank is the problem, I daresay," Edward retorted amiably. "But why aren't you dressed yet? I've spent the day shepherding Emmaline and Rosalind about and yet I've had time to change."

At that Jeremy became very still. He looked at his friend and asked, "I suppose everything is arranged?"

"Everything," Edward agreed. "We are to separate during the fireworks and meet at the Cat and Hound half an hour later. You have heard of it, I presume? Well, Emmaline will accompany Rosalind to the inn so that she need not feel nervous."

"Yes, of course I have heard of it," Jeremy said

quietly. He hesitated then said, "I have been think-ing, Edward. Perhaps we had best call this off."

"Call it off? But what about your father?" Hastings asked disingenuously.

"I shall go to him and tell him the truth," Jeremy said grimly. "He may banish me to the Continent or even carry out his threat to impoverish me. I don't know, the devil take it! But anything is better than this farce."

"What of the Marquess of Alnwick?" Edward asked, trying to suppress his sense of alarm. "You cannot abandon Rosalind to his clutches."

"Damnation! I had forgotten that," Jeremy exclaimed. "Why don't *you* marry her?"

Edward lifted a shoulder gracefully. "But it is you who have led her to believe you meant marriage."

Jeremy regarded his friend shrewdly. "Odd," he said, "I had thought we had agreed you would marry her in the end. Indeed I recall you once said you would do anything to prevent my marriage to Rosalind."

"You had no such scruples last night. As I recall you were quite ready to marry me to Emmaline instead," Edward pointed out grimly. "Don't you think it late for them now?"

"Better now than after committing the folly of eloping with a gently bred young lady," Jeremy flung at him. "As for last night, you knew I was half drunk when you arrived. Indeed, half out of my head before that with the shock of seeing my father and Emmaline's here in London. How could you let me plan such a thing when I was in such a state?"

"Let you?" Edward demanded indignantly. "Will

you tell me how I could have stopped you? In any event you did plan it and the arrangements are all in train. If you cannot bring yourself to go through with the elopement why then you must at least show yourself at the inn and explain matters to Rosalind yourself. I shall not do it for you."

"Why can I not do so at the park?" Jeremy demanded in confusion.

Once more Edward looked alarmed. A moment later, however, he had himself well in hand. "What? Hold such a conversation in a public place? And with my mother there? No, if that is your mood, then perhaps you had best not come at all. Just meet us at the Cat and Hound half an hour after the fireworks begin. Somewhere around ten o'clock, I should suppose. I will make your excuses to the ladies."

"Thank you, but I believe I am able to keep myself in check," Jeremy said with heavy irony. "I shall join you if you will just give me a few minutes to get ready."

"Certainly." Edward said coolly. "But I believe I shall wait for you in the carriage."

Jeremy started toward his dressing room, then stopped. "Edward, what about the Marquess of Alnwick?" he demanded. "If you will not marry her either, what is Miss Kirkwood going to do?"

Edward regarded Jeremy steadily. "If, in the end, you do not change your mind once more and carry her away, why then we shall just have to contrive something else."

"You're a good friend," Jeremy said quietly.

"Just hurry and change your clothes," Edward retorted amiably.

When they reached the Hastings town house,

they discovered that not only were Emmaline and Mrs. Hastings ready, but Sir Osbert and Lady Delwyn and Jeremy's father were as well. Sir Osbert looked very pleased with himself as he said, "Anna, Gilbert, and I decided to join you young people. I hope you do not mind?"

"Of course not, sir," Jeremy said at once. "We are delighted to have you, and to see you in such good health."

"Very prettily said." Lord Barnett nodded approvingly. "Your betrothal to Emmaline has done you a great deal of good, I see. Marriage will no doubt do even more."

Hastily Emmaline said, "We ought to be going. We still have to stop for Rosalind on our way to the park."

"Yes, of course," Mrs. Hastings said with alacrity. "It will not do to have her think we have forgotten her."

On the way, the men rode in one carriage, the ladies in another. Jeremy sat immersed in his own worries. Abruptly, however, he realized his opinion had been asked. "I should like to go to Green Park to see the Castle of Discord," Sir Osbert said. "I have it upon excellent authority that it is to explode and reveal some sort of tower."

"And I should like to see the Chinese pagoda in St. James Park," Lord Barnett countered playfully. "What do you suggest, Jeremy? The ladies refused to make a choice back there, and Edward insists that it is not his place to decide."

Jeremy appeared to consider the matter carefully. Finally he said, "Well, as the castle is not timed to explode until midnight, we might easily do both, going on to Green Park after the fireworks at St. James. I believe that is set to conclude by ten."

"Capital!" Lord Barnett said, rubbing his hands together in satisfaction.

"A Solomon-like reply," Sir Osbert said with quiet amusement. "I bow to your wisdom, as well, Jeremy. When we halt to pick up Emmaline's friend, you may tell the others what we have decided."

So, when the carriages drew to a halt in front of the Kirkwood residence, Jeremy jumped down and approached the carriage with the ladies, quickly telling them the news. Matters were not quite so simple, however, as they had supposed. Lady Kirkwood did not wish to allow Rosalind to go. Tight-lipped, she met Jeremy and Edward on her doorstep and said, "I am sorry, Mr. Barnett, Mr. Hastings, but Rosalind has been pledged to go out tonight with another gentleman. No doubt she forgot to inform you."

Edward's own lips drew into a taut line as he replied, "She did not. But if you consult with Lord Kirkwood, I believe you will find she is to come with us."

That was evidently a facer, Jeremy noted, seeing the lady's look of astonishment and disbelief. No doubt, he thought grimly, it matched his own. In the midst of this discussion Lord Kirkwood appeared on the doorstep himself. "What's this?" he demanded. "Why haven't you all gone to the festivities yet? Is there some problem?"

"They wish Rosalind to go with them," Lady Kirkwood said in frozen accents.

Kirkwood's face darkened. "Do they? Nonsense!"

His eyes met Edward's. "She has been pledged to accompany Miss Delwyn for the past week, you know," Edward said quietly.

For a long moment the two men stared at one another. Then Kirkwood's shoulders sagged and he said, "Well, if she is going, then let her go!"

"But the Marquess of Alnwick?" Lady Kirkwood protested softly to her husband. "He is due sometime this evening and you know how angry he was that Rosalind was out during the day."

"The devil take Alnwick; we will think of something to tell him!" was the furiously whispered reply.

And then Rosalind herself appeared, dressed to go out with a silk shawl about her shoulders. With perfect equanimity Edward handed her into the carriage shared by his mother, Lady Delwyn, and Emmaline.

As they returned to the other carriage Jeremy asked, "How the devil did you manage that, Edward? What did you say to Lord Kirkwood?"

Hastings colored but answered evenly, "I hinted there was another suitor in view, one better placed. I also said that if he did not give that suitor a chance to court his daughter, I would raise a scandal over the affair."

"So tomorrow when he discovers there is no other suitor, he will once again press Rosalind to marry that blackguard?" Jeremy asked heavily.

Edward merely had time to shrug in reply. He did manage to smooth over, however, the questions Sir Osbert and Lord Barnett naturally had over the scene that had just occurred. Fortunately they had not been close enough to hear what was said and Edward fobbed them off with a Banbury tale of warnings to make an early night of it. Soon enough they had reached the vicinity of the park and it was time to leave the carriages and make their way on foot through the press of the crowd to see the pagoda. "It stands some seven stories tall, I hear," Lord Barnett told Mrs. Hastings as he guided her toward the goal.

"Quite right," Edward agreed, "and it stands on a bridge over the canal."

"There it is." Rosalind pointed. "I do believe you can just see the top of it from here."

When they were much closer, they were able to see the Japanese lanterns at the pagoda and the gas jets on the roof. Most of the *ton* had turned out for the spectacle. The time passed quickly in greeting friends and exchanging the latest *on-dits*, one of which was the news of Sir Osbert's marriage. He and Anna delighted in the felicitations of everyone and the exclamations of astonishment at his renewed health.

All too soon the fireworks began. Immediately Rosalind played her part. Drooping against Edward, she said, in a faint voice, "Forgive me, Mrs. Hastings, but suddenly I find that I do not feel well."

"Don't worry, I shall take you home at once," Edward said, picking up his cue. "Miss Delwyn, surely you will accompany us? You may be able to give Miss Kirkwood some comfort."

"Of course," Emmaline said in a tiny voice. "You will excuse us, Mrs. Hastings?"

"Yes, yes," she said impatiently. "And I suppose Jeremy will wish to go as well."

None of the four protested and soon they were making their way out of the park, but not toward the carriages. This time, for the sake of discretion, they wanted to hire a hackney. As they walked, Edward spoke rapidly to Barnett. "You must first go back to your quarters, Jeremy. I left some things there that Rosalind will need. And Emmaline. She does not mean to go back to my mother's house tonight. You must fetch them."

Jeremy's face must have betrayed something of the astonishment he felt, for Rosalind asked innocently, "Do you mean to elope with Edward as well, Emmaline?"

Jeremy did not wait to hear her answer but flung himself away. "I shall meet you at the Cat and Hound within the hour," he called over his shoulder. "You are to go nowhere until I arrive," he told Emmaline and Edward grimly.

Her face very pale, Emmaline could do nothing but follow her friends to the street, where Edward quickly procured one of the hackneys hanging about hoping for fares. Nor did the fellow so much as blink when Edward gave as their destination the name of the posting house for the North road.

"Thank goodness for the stolid lack of curiosity of such fellows," Edward said with a sigh of relief as they settled themselves in the carriage. He turned to Rosalind and said earnestly, "Now, Miss Kirkwood, it will take a little time to get there but you must not be nervous. Between us we have arranged everything and soon all will be well."

"I cannot like an elopement," she replied gravely, "but it seems the only answer. I wonder what marriage to Jeremy will be like."

"Interesting, I haven't the slightest doubt," Edward told her coolly.

Emmaline leaned farther and farther back into the shadows of the carriage, unwilling to have either of her companions see her face. She was very much afraid that something of her distress must be showing, and indeed, if Rosalind's faintness earlier had been feigned, Emmaline's own was now very real.

19

THE Delwyns, Lord Barnett, and Mrs. Hastings were still watching the fireworks when suddenly the pagoda burst into flames and toppled over into the water. Sir Osbert was the first to realize that this had not been part of the planned spectacle. He immediately confided his suspicions to the others and said, "We had best get out of here before the crowd realizes what is afoot and gives way to panic."

As a result, they were well away before the general exodus began. Mrs. Hastings was somewhat surprised to discover that her son had taken neither carriage, but was inclined to put it down to a filial concern that his elders not be crowded into one. "I think I should like to go back to the Kirkwood house first, before we go on to Green Park," Sir Osbert said to Mrs. Hastings as he handed her into her carriage. "To collect Emmaline, if she is still there."

"An excellent notion," Mrs. Hastings said approvingly. "I shall come along as well since Edward will no doubt be with her."

In spite of his earlier foresight, Sir Osbert had no suspicion of what was about to occur. He and

Barnett discussed instead the pagoda and speculated upon how many persons might have been injured. Anna had chosen to ride with Mrs. Hastings, the two ladies well on their way to becoming fast friends, and they discussed the forthcoming wedding between Emmaline and Jeremy. Mrs. Hastings said nothing to disillusion her companion, for it was her sincere hope that the wedding would take place so that she need no longer worry about her son and his involvement with Miss Delwyn.

When they reached the Kirkwood household, it was Sir Osbert who left the carriage and rapped upon the door, which was immediately opened. "I believe Miss Kirkwood returned, sometime since, and I wonder if my daughter, Miss Delwyn, who was with her is still here."

The footman looked a trifle startled. "But Miss Kirkwood has not yet returned," he replied.

"Are you certain?" Sir Osbert asked, somewhat taken aback. "Please do me the favor to go and check with your mistress. Perhaps you simply did not see her return."

The footman's face betrayed none of his outrage at the suggestions that he might have been remiss in his duties. Instead he bowed and said, "If you will come inside, I shall endeavor to see if her ladyship will speak with you."

Delwyn did so. After what seemed an interminable time Lady Kirkwood appeared. "Sir Osbert?" she asked. He nodded and she went on, "My footman tells me that you expected to find my daughter here. But you must know she has gone out with yours."

"Yes, yes," Sir Osbert said impatiently, "but she

was not feeling quite the thing and my daughter Emmaline, Edward Hastings, and Jeremy Barnett all volunteered to bring her back here. That was some time ago."

"Perhaps they were delayed, their carriage caught up by the crowds," Lady Kirkwood suggested.

"Perhaps," Sir Osbert agreed doubtfully, "though our own had no difficulty reaching here."

"Perhaps you would care to wait for your daughter to arrive?" Lady Kirkwood offered reluctantly.

"Yes, yes I should," Sir Osbert agreed readily. "Will you excuse me while I inform my companions?"

"Of course," she said graciously.

The footman held the door open while Sir Osbert quickly went down the steps and spoke to Mrs. Hastings. "It appears that they have not yet gotten here," he told her. "I mean to wait until they do."

"Perhaps they went to my house," Mrs. Hastings suggested sensibly. "I shall go there, and if they did I shall send word round to you straightaway."

"Thank you," Sir Osbert said warmly. "Barnett will no doubt accompany you so that you need not brave the streets alone."

Anna reached out her hand to her husband and asked, "What should you like me to do, my love? Wait here with you or go with Mrs. Hastings?"

"Wait here with me," he answered promptly.

She stepped out of the carriage to join her husband just as Lord Barnett came up to them, drawn by curiosity. "What the devil is going on?" he asked.

Quickly Sir Osbert put him in possession of the facts and he agreed with alacrity to accompany Mrs. Hastings home. "You keep the other carriage here," he said, "in the event they do return and then you can come join us. I doubt very much a hackney cab can be found tonight except near the parks where they are all hanging about hoping for fares."

Sir Osbert nodded curtly then escorted his wife inside leaving Barnett to speak to both coachmen. Lady Kirkwood was startled, to be sure, by the appearance of Sir Osbert's wife, but she was too well bred to protest. "Of course you are welcome," she said graciously. "Won't you come into the drawing room." She paused then asked, in a more natural voice, "Tell me, Lady Delwyn, have we met before? You seem very familiar."

Anna regarded her hostess shrewdly. "We met, perhaps, the year you came out," she said, "though I am surprised you remember. I fear I was some years older and you were by far the prettier."

Lady Kirkwood flushed with pleasure and with genuine warmth said, "Do sit down, my dear, and allow me to ring for some tea. Then we can enjoy a comfortable coze together."

Unfortunately, the others soon discovered that the party of young people had not gone back to the Hastings household either. Instead, Mrs. Hastings and Lord Barnett reached the town house and found Emmaline's maid waiting with a note in her hand. "I went to draw back the covers of her bed since she had told me not to wait up for her and I discovered this," she explained as she placed the missive in Mrs. Hastings' hand then left the room.

It was addressed to that lady and she wasted no time in opening it. Lord Barnett seated himself opposite and waited for her to read it. When she was done, Mrs. Hastings crumpled the note and said to Barnett in a voice that was scarcely above a whisper, "I was afraid of this. They have done it. My son and Miss Delwyn have run off together."

"Nonsense," Barnett said sharply as he came to his feet. "That is absurd. Miss Delwyn is to marry my son. They are in love with one another."

"That is what I thought," Mrs. Hastings retorted. "Until Emmaline disabused me of the notion. She has fallen out of love with your son and into love with mine. But she has been afraid to tell you or her father because of the shock to his system and your threat to your son."

"Nonsense," Barnett repeated. His face was a trifle pale, however, as he added, "I had no desire for the poor girl to be driven to lengths such as this. But are you sure?"

"See for yourself," Mrs. Hastings said in tragic accents then burst into tears. Gingerly Barnett read the note aloud:

My Dear Mrs. Hastings,
    You have been very kind to me, but I can no longer stay under your roof. You need have no fear, however. Edward will see me safely into my father's care after we have done what we must. Whatever occurs, you must not be angry with Rosalind and Jeremy. Later, I shall send round for my things. By then everyone will understand that marriage between myself and Jeremy is out of the question. In view of your many kindnesses to me, I could not bear to face you again, after this. I remain, however,

                              Respectfully yours,
                              Emmaline Delwyn

"There! You see?" Mrs. Hastings sobbed again.

"What else can she mean save that she cannot face me after running off with my son. And no doubt Jeremy and Rosalind are helping them. That is why the girl was not at the Kirkwood household."

Lord Barnett was not entirely convinced. He said as much, then added hastily as a fresh wave of crying overtook the lady, "Well, but even if it is true, whatever are we to do about it? We haven't the slightest clue as to where they have gone."

"The North road, I've no doubt," she retorted impatiently. "Headed for Gretna Green. It is just the sort of thing that might seem romantic to a foolish girl like Emmaline."

"Why don't you ask her maid if she knows anything," Barnett suggested reasonably. "If she does, it will save us a great deal of trouble."

Fortunately, Mary had anticipated that she might be wanted and in a matter of minutes she stood facing the pair after making a neat little curtsy. "Yes, ma'am. She did say that she meant to go to her father. But I overheard her say that first she would be going to the Cat and Hound Inn. She was talking to herself and didn't see me and I thought that odd enough that I ought to remember it."

"You see?" Mrs. Hastings demanded of Barnett. "That's right on the North road. We must go after them at once. Yes, and send word round to her father at the Kirkwoods. Perhaps he can talk some sense into her even if we cannot. Come, hurry! There may yet be time to stop this folly."

Barnett could not have disobeyed even had he wished to, and he did not wish to. Bitterly he noted that this was more than a little his own fault for pressing his son and Emmaline into a betrothal that neither obviously had wanted. If they caught up with the eloping pair, at least he could tell Emmaline that he would no longer force the point with his son and that she was therefore not obliged to take such a disastrous step.

The carriage, which had been sent to the stables, was soon brought round again and the two on their way. A boy had already been dispatched with a note for Sir Osbert. Grimly Barnett wondered what his friend would say when he learned what was afoot.

As it turned out, Sir Osbert almost did not. It was a different footman who opened the door to the boy with the message and he thought the lad had mistaken the house. Only when the boy hotly insisted that Sir Osbert was inside did the noise bring the first footman, who immediately recognized the name and accepted the note. He lost no time in presenting it to the gentleman involved.

With a frown, Sir Osbert accepted the missive the footman held out to him and said to Lady Kirkwood and his wife, a trifle uneasily, "Pray excuse me. Perhaps it is word that the young people are all at Mrs. Hastings' home."

He read rapidly, turning paler by the moment. To the two ladies he said shakily, "Forgive me. I must be off at once."

"What is it?" Anna asked with concern.

"Mischief, I've no doubt. Is there mention of my daughter as well?" Lady Kirkwood said icily.

"I'm afraid there is," Sir Osbert said quietly. "An elopement is afoot. Mrs. Hastings and Lord Barnett are on their way to stop it—as shall I in a few moments."

At once Anna was on her feet. "I'll come too," she said. "My presence may help to allay gossip. We are fortunate in that everyone will be out late tonight at the celebrations and it will not seem odd if we are seen returning home past midnight. Does the note say where we are to go?"

"The Cat and Hound Inn," he said grimly.

"On the North road!" Lady Kirkwood cried, fanning herself rapidly. "I knew it! Rosalind is eloping with Edward Hastings and your daughter and Jeremy Barnett are helping them. I knew there would be trouble! And my husband not even here to help. What shall I do?"

Sir Osbert spoke quietly. "The note merely says that I am to meet Barnett and Mrs. Hastings to prevent an elopement. Perhaps Emmaline is eloping with Jeremy."

"Why should she do that?" Anna asked in bewilderment. "They have both your blessing and Lord Barnett's."

"Yes why should they do that. No, sir, you are mistaken," Lady Kirkwood said in stentorian tones. "Hastings came just this morning to tell my husband that in the face of our own plans for Rosalind, he meant to court her. When my husband refused permission, he laughed and made threats of scandal if we did not allow him to see her. But we never dreamed he would go so far as to elope! Though I own I wish you were right. Let me send for Rosalind's maid and see if she left us a note."

A few minutes later that girl curtsied meekly to the three and said, when asked, "No, m'lady. She did say, though, that if you are to wonder, I should tell you that she might not be home when you expected."

As Lady Kirkwood pressed a hand to her now-feverish brow Sir Osbert said firmly, "Anna and I must be off, Lady Kirkwood. You are not to worry about a thing. We shall catch up with them and bring your daughter home to you straightaway, and I promise you there will be no scandal. When your husband returns, you may tell him so."

20

EMMALINE paced the floor of the small parlor
Edward had thoughtfully bespoken at the Cat and
Hound. It did not ease her agitation that both
Rosalind and Edward appeared to be entirely calm.
They were only waiting, Edward had said, until
Jeremy arrived for the final arrangements to be
made and everyone to be on their way.

Jeremy, when he did arrive, looked even paler
than Emmaline. He brought the parcels that Edward had sent him for into the room and then
looked at Rosalind. That young lady rose to her
feet but did not even blush in the slightest as she
placed a gentle hand on his arm and said, "I know
we must be leaving soon and I assure you I shall
be ready in a trice. But there is something I must
do first and I pray you will excuse me."

Jeremy would have stopped her but Edward
was also on his feet and saying, "I shall go see
to everything, Jeremy, so that there need be
no delay."

Then they were both gone from the room and
Emmaline and Jeremy were left to face one another. She could not bear it, however, and turned
away. Faintly she said, "I must wish you well on

your journey, Jeremy, and hope that this will solve both your problems and Rosalind's. I hope you will be happy together."

"And you?" he demanded roughly from behind her. "I suppose you are to elope with Edward? And that is why there is a parcel here for you as well as for Rosalind?"

She backed away from him. "No, of course not!" she cried. "How could you think such a thing?"

Jeremy regarded her insolently. With cool deliberation he sat down, put his feet up on another chair, and said, "Oh? Then you have other plans? Perhaps you mean to simply run away with this . . . this man you claim to love?" She shook her head and he went on tauntingly, "Why not? Because you value your independence too highly? Or because you think he will not marry you?"

"I know he will not," she replied, her voice scarcely above a whisper.

"I think you will find you are mistaken. I have spoken to him myself," Jeremy answered, leaning his chair back so that he could see her face.

At that Emmaline turned to meet his eyes squarely, rage beginning to flame inside her. "You utter fool!" she hissed at him. "You utterly arrogant fool! I wish I may never set eyes on you again!"

Then she ran toward the door, meaning to go anywhere so long as she escaped from his presence. The chair scraped the floor as she spoke and Jeremy was right behind her as she reached for the handle. Just as she tried to open the door there was the unmistakable sound of a key turning in the lock and the sound of two voices laughing from the other side of the door. Rosalind's words came first. "Now you shall have to work out matters between you," she said.

"And we shan't let you out until you do," Edward added firmly.

"What about the elopement?" Emmaline demanded frantically.

"I shall take care of everything," Edward replied coolly, "but there isn't going to be an elopement and you might ask Jeremy why."

Again there was laughter and then the sound of footsteps moving away. Both Emmaline and Jeremy pounded on the door but to no avail. "He must have bribed the innkeeper quite well," Jeremy observed grimly when they gave up at last. Then, in a voice that dripped contempt, he goaded her, "And this is the man you love?"

Emmaline backed away. "I never said he was the man I loved," she flung at him.

"No?" Jeremy leaned his shoulders against the door. "Who else?" She did not reply and he laughed harshly. "You haven't even the courage to admit it. Why not? Pride? Because he helped to lock you in this room with me?"

"Pride?" she countered. "What about you? Haven't you any anger that Edward has thwarted your marriage to Rosalind?"

He shrugged and said carelessly, "Oh, but I never claimed there was love in that. You know as well as I that the elopement was a means of saving both the lady and myself from a worse fate."

"Ah, yes, marriage to me," Emmaline observed bitterly.

At that Jeremy hurled an oath and crossed the

room to grasp her arms and shake her as he said roughly, "You forget, my dear, that you were the one to end our betrothal."

Somehow Emmaline wrenched herself free. Retreating, she flung at him, "Oh, yes. I recall how keen you were for the match. How you so eagerly set a date for the wedding vows and proclaimed it to everyone who asked. No doubt you always go pale and flinch when you are deliriously happy as you were when people congratulated us upon the betrothal."

The table was between them now, and both were breathing heavily. Jeremy laughed harshly as he said, "How touching. Next I suppose you will tell me you broke off the betrothal for my sake?"

"No, for my own!" she flung back at him.

"Why?" he taunted her. "Because I was such an ogre toward you? Because you heard too many tales of my past conduct and that terrified your little Puritan heart and you could not bear to be shackled to me? What were you afraid of, my dear? That I would force you to attend my orgies? If so, you mistook me. I should have held my orgies quite distinct from our household."

"You dare to boast of it?" she demanded incredulously.

"Why not?" he asked coolly, advancing around the table toward her.

Emmaline moved further away. "If this is what you intend, I can only be grateful Edward has prevented your elopement. You are worse than the Marquess of Alnwick."

"Oh come, come," he chided her. "Surely not

that. After all, unlike Alnwick, I should never force unwelcome attentions upon my wife, only my mistresses. What could there be for a wife to object to in that?"

Shaking with rage and close to tears, Emmaline said, "I hate you! You are completely incapable of understanding how a wife would feel. If she loved you, that would hurt more than if you did force your attentions on her." Resentfully she could not keep from adding, "You probably wouldn't even know if they were unwelcome to her or not."

Jeremy, who had continued to move around the table, halted abruptly and regarded Emmaline with a puzzled look to his glittering eyes. "Indeed?" he asked softly. "And is that what you were afraid of? That I should take too many mistresses? That would have distressed you? Beyond the matter of your pride?"

In panic, Emmaline turned her eyes away from him. "I—I . . . it is nothing to me what you do. We were speaking of Rosalind, weren't we?"

Because she had looked away, Emmaline did not see him swiftly close the distance between them until he reached out and imprisoned her wrists with his hands. Softly, his eyes still glittering dangerously at her, Jeremy said, "*I* was asking why you chose to break off our betrothal."

Vainly Emmaline tried to break free but his grip was like iron. Panting, she demanded, "What does it matter why I broke our betrothal? All that matters is that I have."

"So that you can turn to Edward? Where were you going tonight? For you cannot deny that you meant to go somewhere. And with Edward, for he would not have let you go alone," Jeremy demanded harshly. "Why? Because he does not frighten you as I do? Because you think *he* does not have mistresses? You are in for a surprise there, my dear." He paused, then demanded more softly, "Or is it that he doesn't frighten you because he does not make you feel like this?"

And then his lips were on hers, demanding the response he knew would come. As always, a wave of longing swept over her and Emmaline could not help but sway toward Jeremy. One hand freed her right wrist and went around her waist, imprisoning her against the length of his body. With horror she realized she could feel the evidence of his desire pressed intimately against her. As though she were drowning, Emmaline clung to him, lost to all sense of time, all sense of propriety.

It was Jeremy who broke the embrace. "Damn you," he said, looking down at her. "I won't let you marry Edward. I don't care how safe he makes you feel. You'll marry me if I have to keep you locked in this room all night to convince you! And then we'll go and tell my father. He'll be delighted, you may be sure."

Emmaline felt as though a tub of cold water had been dashed over her. His father. Of course. With the elopement to Rosalind thwarted he must make sure of a wife before he next saw his father. All this had nothing to do with her; Jeremy was simply very skilled in lovemaking. She ought to have remembered that, for everyone had been at such pains to tell her so.

As though he sensed the change in her, Jeremy let go of Emmaline and looked at her, a puzzled expression on his face. She had gone pale and utterly listless, and instead of reacting either with favor or anger to his words, she merely sat in the nearest chair and said tonelessly, "No Jeremy, I shan't marry you. It doesn't matter how long you keep me here. But if you wish, I'll speak to your father and tell him the betrothal is broken and that it is not your fault."

"He won't believe you," Jeremy could not help but say. "But that is beside the point."

Slowly Emmaline shook her head. "No, that is precisely the point. You don't wish to marry me any more tonight than you did when he first proposed the match."

"You seem very certain of that," Jeremy replied harshly.

Still not looking at him, she said dully, "I am. Oh, I'll allow you almost convinced me. You are very skilled at what you do. But I know very well that if it were not for your father's command and his threat to leave you to starve, you would not wish for marriage. And certainly not marriage to me."

Finally she raised her eyes to look at him but Jeremy had turned away and was regarding the fireplace fixedly. For a long time he did not answer, but when he did he said quietly, "And if it were different? If I had truly wished to marry you? Would you have found the notion so distasteful?"

It was madness to reply with honesty but tonight Emmaline felt drunk with madness. Noth-

ing seemed to matter as she said, "If that had
been so, I would have wed you with all my heart
and spent my life in loving you."

Jeremy whirled around, hope in his eyes, only
to have the grimness once more possess him as he
saw the finality in her face. And so it ended, he
thought, as he cursed himself as a fool for so
badly bungling matters ever since the beginning.

21

BARNETT and Mrs. Hastings reached the inn first. Discreet questioning of the owner of the Cat and Hound brought the welcome news that the persons they sought were still there. "If you will follow me," the innkeeper said with a bow, "I shall take you to the parlor where your young friends are waiting."

Grimly the two did as they were bid. Grimness, however, turned to astonishment as the door of the private parlor opened and they found themselves facing only Edward and Rosalind. "Where is my son?" Barnett demanded as soon as the innkeeper had left them alone.

"Where is Emmaline?" Mrs. Hastings demanded of *her* son. "Aren't you eloping with her?"

Edward regarded the angry pair calmly. To Lord Barnett he said, holding out something to that gentleman, "You will find your son and Miss Delwyn down the hall. Third door on the right. Here is the key to that parlor."

Without further explanation he waited for Lord Barnett to go and the gentleman did so with a bow to Mrs. Hastings. Edward then turned to Rosalind and, taking her hand, said with perfect equanimity, "There is no elopement, Mama. I am, however, taking Miss Kirkwood tonight to stay with Aunt Theresa for a few weeks until I have come to terms with her father. You may as well know that we are going to be married."

Mrs Hastings promptly fainted.

Lord Barnett, at precisely the same moment, was unlocking the door to the parlor that Edward Hastings had indicated. As he did so, he saw Sir Osbert and his wife Anna hurrying toward him. Without words they entered to find Emmaline and Jeremy at opposite sides of the room, refusing to look at one another. Bewildered, Sir Osbert said, "Where are young Hastings and Miss Kirkwood?"

"In the other parlor," Lord Barnett answered curtly. Sir Osbert turned to go to them but Barnett stopped him. "In a moment," he said. "First, I should like you to hear what I am going to say to Emmaline." Moving to where she stood, he took her hands in his and said, "My dear child, I have come to tell you that I have changed my mind. You need not marry Jeremy. You have made me realize that I must not force him to the altar with my threats."

As Emmaline tried to choke out a thank-you, Sir Osbert strode into the center of the room, his cane all but forgotten as he demanded, "What the devil are you talking about, Gilbert? Of course they are to be married."

Lord Barnett looked at his old friend and said heavily, "No. Your daughter was prepared to run off with young Hastings rather than do so."

"What?" Sir Osbert demanded incredulously.

"You must have windmills in your head! Edward Hastings was eloping with Miss Kirkwood."

As the two older men glared at one another Jeremy coughed discreetly, drawing their attention. "Actually," he said hesitantly, "*I* was to elope with Miss Kirkwood. Both of us, it seems, realized our mistake, however, before committing such a folly."

Sir Osbert's face was gray as he turned to his daughter and said, "My poor Emmaline. I never meant this to happen to you. What a devil of a thing for you to face."

Emmaline took his hand and forced herself to smile as she said, "It's all right, Papa."

"But why didn't you tell me that matters had gone awry between you?" he asked in bewilderment.

"I thought you were still very ill," she replied softly, "and I had no wish to distress you."

As father and daughter embraced, Lord Barnett had the grace to look abashed as he turned to his son. "I am sorry, Jeremy," he said with uncharacteristic gentleness. "In meaning the best for you, it seems I have only succeeded in making a muddle of everything. And in misjudging you. Mrs. Hastings has been giving me the sharp edge of her tongue, as we came here, telling me that you are far more of a man than I have ever given you credit for."

Jeremy would have spoken then, but he was forestalled by the appearance of Mrs. Hastings with her son Edward and Rosalind. A trifle shakily Mrs. Hastings announced, "It appears that my son and Miss Kirkwood are soon to be betrothed." Ignoring the hasty exclamations, she went on, "The three of us are leaving now to take Miss Kirkwood to my sister Theresa's house where she will be staying until the wedding."

Sir Osbert spoke blankly. "But Lady Kirkwood expects me to bring her back home tonight. She believes the two of them are eloping."

"I am afraid it will not be possible for Miss Kirkwood to return home just yet," Edward said grimly as he patted Rosalind's hand reassuringly. "Not until her father and I have had a chance to speak and he listens to reason. I will not have Rosalind betrothed to anyone against her will."

"Or kept from the betrothal against my will," Rosalind added shyly.

Jeremy was the first to recover. With long strides he crossed the room and kissed Rosalind's hand. "My warmest felicitations," he told her. Then turning to Edward, he said severely, "You wretched fellow! And not a word of it to me except to pretend to aid me in this sham elopement. What the devil were you about, taking part in such nonsense?"

"You would not listen to reason," Edward answered mildly. Then, looking past his friend he said, "Emmaline? Won't you wish us well?"

Forcing a smile, she replied warmly, "Of course I shall. It has been my dearest wish to see Rosalind happy and I know that she will be with you."

As she spoke Emmaline embraced her friend and added softly, "Now you need never be afraid of your parents or the Marquess of Alnwick again."

She would have pulled back then, but Rosalind held tightly on to her friend's hands as she asked sternly, "And you? Have you and Jeremy worked matters out between you?"

Emmaline shook her head and would have denied it when she suddenly felt an arm go around her waist. From beside her she heard Jeremy's voice reply smoothly, "Why, I don't doubt our wedding will follow close upon the heels of your own. Unless, of course, my father can help me obtain a special license, in which case we will dance at yours as a married couple."

In shock Emmaline tried to pull her hands free of Rosalind's and her waist free of Jeremy's imprisoning arm but neither would let go. Frantically she looked up at Jeremy, conscious that Rosalind's eyes were dancing as she said, "I knew that if we tricked you, matters would work out between you. That is all Edward and I have stayed to hear."

"But we aren't going to be married," Emmaline finally managed to protest.

"Of course we are," Jeremy retorted sternly. Then, pulling her closer to him, he added to the others, a hint of laughter in his voice, "Don't worry, I shall soon school her not to contradict me in front of my friends, shan't I, my love?" Then he looked down at Emmaline with a warmth that threatened to shatter her completely.

Mrs. Hastings broke the silence that followed that outrageousness by saying firmly, "If the two of you wish to spend the rest of the night billing and cooing, that is up to you, but we must be on our way. Theresa is expecting us and I still have to dispatch Lady Kirkwood a note explaining what is afoot. I don't doubt she'll be angry but she is not such a nodcock as to cause a scandal when we have offered her a way out of it."

The next few minutes were occupied with leave-taking and Emmaline tried to ignore the arm about her waist that did not once slacken. When the three had gone, however, it was time for Emmaline and Jeremy to face their fathers.

"What the devil is going on?" Lord Barnett demanded. "I have said you need not get married, Jeremy."

"Unhand my daughter," Sir Osbert said, restraining his temper with great effort. "She has already told us she does not wish to marry you."

He would have said more had Anna not laid a hand on his arm and warned him with her eyes to be still. Meanwhile Emmaline could not bring herself to look at any of them and she tried instead to break free. "You heard my father, let me go," she said, pounding her fists upon Jeremy's chest.

Without effort he imprisoned her hands with one of his own, the other arm still tight about her waist. The laughter in his voice was even more pronounced as he said, "Oh, no, my little vixen, not until you set a date for our wedding."

"I told you I won't," she retorted, looking up at Jeremy. "Have you forgotten what I said already?"

Too late she realized her mistake as she felt herself go weak under his gaze. A smile played about his lips as he replied coolly, "I have forgotten nothing." As she colored he went on, "You said that you would not marry me because I was doing so at my father's command. You said that if, instead, I was asking you to marry me of my own free will, you would do so with all your heart and love. Well? You do not see my father threatening me anymore. You do not see your father pressing for the match. Indeed, I think they are all but ready to hang me for suggesting such a thing."

If Jeremy's voice quivered with laughter, Osbert's

quivered with rage as he said, "Emmaline, you will not marry this fellow. I refuse to allow such a match to take place!"

Barnett's voice was close behind as he said, "I warn you, Jeremy, if you try to force Emmaline to this match, which is so evidently distasteful to her, I shall cut you off without a penny!"

Jeremy let go Emmaline's hands and tilted up her chin to make her meet his eyes, laughing outright as he said, "You see? I fear it is Gretna Green for us, after all. But at least now you cannot accuse me of motives other than love when I tell you that I mean to marry you."

This time Emmaline did not try to keep from swaying against him as she grew weaker still under the warmth of his gaze. "Well?" he demanded impatiently. "Is it Gretna Green or do I carry you off to a room somewhere and keep you my prisoner until you do agree to marry me?"

In spite of herself, Emmaline laughed, oblivious to the expressions of outrage from behind them. "Of course I shall marry you," she told him softly. "Thought I cannot begin to understand why you want to, after all."

"Can't you?" he asked softly, before he bent his head to kiss her.

Behind them the cries of "Stop that this instant!" grew louder.

After a moment they broke their embrace and Emmaline said impishly, "They are quite right, Jeremy. If we are going to Gretna Green, we had best be on our way. I wonder if there is a carriage here we might hire?"

"I quite think so," Jeremy replied with a seriousness that was belied by the laughter in his eyes.

Hastily the elder Barnett moved to block the door. "You will do nothing of the sort," he said.

"Not unless you wish to drive me into my grave, after all," Sir Osbert told his daughter querulously.

For the first time Anna spoke. She crossed the room, tilted Emmaline's chin to make the girl look at her. "It is too bad of you to tease your fathers like this. You know very well there is no need to fly to Gretna Green. All Sir Osbert wishes is your happiness, Emmaline," she said. Looking at Jeremy, she added, "Once he is brought round to see that this reprobate is truly the person you wish to wed, he will grant his permission readily enough."

Jeremy laughed. "Now I see why Sir Osbert married you, Lady Delwyn. Such a combination of beauty and wisdom in one woman!"

Grumbling, Sir Osbert also crossed the room to his daughter. Looking directly into her eyes, he said, "Do you really wish to marry this fellow, Emmaline? If you don't, I swear I shall see to it that he does not bother you again."

"Yes, I do wish it," she replied softly.

Sir Osbert turned to his friend Lord Barnett and said heavily, "Well, what shall we do? I see no alternative but to give our blessing to the match."

The elder Barnett nodded. "But you will not," he told his son sternly, "do anything so scandalous as to elope to Gretna Green. There will be a church wedding on our home estate, just as there ought to be. Is that understood?"

Jeremy met his father's gaze levelly. "What I understand," he said coolly, "is that we shall be married when and where Emmaline wishes it." He paused and looked down at her with a warmth that once more caused her knees to feel weak.

"Well, my love?" he asked her. "What is it to be? Gretna Green? Or London? Or my father's estate?"

She leaned against him as she replied softly, "Anywhere, my love, so long as it is soon."

Lord Barnett and Sir Osbert immediately fell to making plans. Jeremy regarded them grimly for a long moment before he said, "Out. All of you out. No doubt it will shortly be time for you to return to the Clarendon and take Emmaline with you, but before you do, I wish to speak with her alone. Out."

The older men bristled at the tone of command but Anna proved once more Jeremy's ally. "You had best do as he says," she said reasonably. "It is by far the quickest way to put an end to all this and allow us to be on our way." As the three of them left the parlor she turned to admonish the young pair one last time. "Five minutes and not a moment more, do you hear? I shall not allow you to compromise your respectability!"

When the door closed behind the three, Jeremy once more pulled Emmaline to him, kissing her hungrily. At last he broke free and murmured into her hair, "You cannot know how long I have wished to do that without you ripping up at me! Emmaline, we have both been such bloody fools that I thought you would drive me to madness. I shall never let you go again."

"What? You mean to be a tyrant?" she demanded laughingly.

His arms tightened about her. "No, no, I swear I shall try to make you happy," he said.

"And no mistresses?" Emmaline asked disingenuously. Jeremy growled down at her and she pressed on, avoiding his eyes, "I only ask because

I was *so* disappointed when you said you would not invite me to your orgies."

"If I ever catch you at an orgy—" he told her angrily.

"You'll what?" she demanded, looking up at him provocatively.

"Thrash you to within an inch of your life!" he growled before possessing himself once again of her lips with his own.

22

EMMALINE stood staring at him, a look that might have been fear etched upon her face in the flickering candlelight. Behind her, she was all too well aware, the bed lay waiting for them. Jeremy moved closer, his voice quietly determined as he said, "I warned you, madam, and now you must pay the price."

Then, without another word, his hand reached out, grasped the front edge of her gown and ripped it open to the floor. Jerking it free of her, Jeremy flung it to the far corner of the room. Emmaline quivered as he moved closer, his arms reaching around her, imprisoning her against the length of his body. As his dressing gown fell open she could feel the evidence of his desire for her pressed against the triangle between her legs and she moaned.

Jeremy did not wait but lifted her at once and carried her to the bed, flinging her down, throwing off his robe, and then joining her, trapping her body beneath his own. One hand traced a curve of her cheek while the other made free of the globes of her breasts. She gasped as fingers stroked her nipples then trailed downward toward her most private of places. "N-no," she whispered softly.

"No?" Jeremy echoed with eyes that glittered. "Do you mean you would prefer this? Or this?"

She gasped again as his hands stroked her in different ways and she felt the waves of longing once more seizing her. Hesitantly her own hands reached out to touch Jeremy, his chest, his back, his very masculinity. "What—what are you doing to me?" she demanded as reason threatened to desert her.

He laughed softly, some would have said menacingly. "I warned you, madam," he repeated. "I told you that you would lose all sense of who you were when I made love to you. I warned you that the longer you made me wait, on this our wedding day, the more impatient I would become. And now you suffer the consequences, my beloved."

And before she could speak he covered her lips with his own, possessing them, persuading them, seducing them until her arms were tight around his neck and her moans were moans of impatience that matched his own. And then he possessed all of her, riding her with a gentleness that soon wiped out all memory of the brief pain that had come with possession. Together they crested, crying out each other's names at the same moment. Then, together, they rode the wave down until they lay in each other's arms in quiet contentment.

"Is it like this for everyone?" Emmaline asked, at last, in quiet awe.

Amusement tinged Jeremy's voice as he replied, "Would that it were, my love."

Raising herself up on one elbow to look at him,

Emmaline asked accusingly, "Is it this way when you are with your mistresses?"

Growling an oath, Jeremy caught her to him and kissed her thoroughly. "I have no mistresses now," he told her. "Nor do I think I am likely to have need of them while I am wed to you. But if you so much as mention the word again I'll—"

"You'll what?" she asked, eyes dancing.

Very deliberately he traced the shape of her breasts with an errant finger before he replied, "I shall be forced to prove to you that I have no need of anyone else."

Then, as she laughed joyously, Jeremy once more claimed his bride.

About the Author

April Lynn Kihlstrom was born in Buffalo, New York, and graduated from Cornell University with an M.S. in Operations Research. She, her husband, and their two children enjoy traveling and have lived in Paris, Honolulu, Georgia, and New Jersey. When not writing, April Lynn Kihlstrom enjoys needlework and devotes her time to handicapped children.

Ⓞ SIGNET REGENCY ROMANCE   (0451)

WILLFUL BEAUTIES, DASHING LORDS

☐ THE REPENTANT REBEL by Jane Ashford.	(131959—$2.50)
☐ A RADICAL ARRANGEMENT by Jane Ashford.	(125150—$2.25)
☐ THE MARCHINGTON SCANDAL by Jane Ashford.	(142152—$2.50)
☐ THE THREE GRACES by Jane Ashford.	(145844—$2.50)
☐ THE IRRESOLUTE RIVALS by Jane Ashford.	(135199—$2.50)
☐ MY LADY DOMINO by Sandra Heath.	(126149—$2.25)
☐ MALLY by Sandra Heath.	(143469—$2.50)
☐ THE OPERA DANCER by Sandra Heath.	(143531—$2.50)
☐ THE UNWILLING HEIRESS by Sandra Heath.	(145208—$2.50)
☐ MANNERBY'S LADY by Sandra Heath.	(144392—$2.50)
☐ THE SHERBORNE SAPPHIRES by Sandra Heath.	(145860—$2.50)
☐ A PERFECT LIKELESS by Sandra Health.	(135679—$2.50)
☐ LADY JANE'S RIBBONS by Sandra Heath.	(147049—$2.50)
☐ MAKESHIFT MARRIAGE by Sandra Heath.	(147073—$2.50)
☐ FASHION'S LADY by Sandra Heath.	(149130—$2.50)
☐ THE CHADWICK RING by Julia Jefferies.	(142276—$2.50)

Prices slightly higher in Canada.

**Buy them at your local
bookstore or use coupon
on next page for ordering.**

ON SALE NOW!

a realm of romance and passion—the first of Signet's Sup

Ⓞ

ROMANTIC INTERLUDES

- [ ] **THE DEMON RAKE by Gayle Buck** (146093—$2.50)
- [ ] **THE CLERGYMAN'S DAUGHTER by Julia Jeffries** (146115—$2.50)
- [ ] **THE CLOISONNE LOCKET by Barbara Hazard** (145658—$2.50)
- [ ] **THE WOOD NYMPH by Mary Balogh** (146506—$2.50)
- [ ] **THE HEIRS OF BELAIR by Ellen Fitzgerald** (146514—$2.50)
- [ ] **THE DUKE'S GAMBIT by Roberta Eckert** (146522—$2.50)
- [ ] **THE MARQUIS TAKES A BRIDE by Marion Chesney** (146530—$2.50)
- [ ] **LADY JANE'S RIBBONS by Sandra Heath** (147049—$2.50)
- [ ] **THE MAKESHIFT MARRIAGE by Sandra Heath** (147073—$2.50)
- [ ] **FASHION'S LADY by Sandra Heath** (149130—$2.50)
- [ ] **THE WICKED WAGER by Margaret Summerville** (147057—$2.50)
- [ ] **MISTRESS OF THE HUNT by Amanda Scott** (147065—$2.50)
- [ ] **THE RELUCTANT RAKE by Jane Ashford** (148088—$2.50)
- [ ] **THE FALSE FIANCEE by Emma Lange** (148118—$2.50)
- [ ] **THE PROUD VISCOUNT by Laura Matthews** (148096—$2.50)
- [ ] **A VERY PROPER WIDOW by Laura Matthews** (148126—$2.50)

Buy them at your local bookstore or use this convenient coupon for ordering.

NEW AMERICAN LIBRARY,
P.O. Box 999 Bergenfield, New Jersey 07621

Please send me the books I have checked above. I am enclosing $_____
(please add $1.00 to this order to cover postage and handling). Send check
or money order—no cash or C.O.D.'s. Prices and numbers are subject to change
without notice.

Name _____

Address_____

City_____State_____Zip Code_____
Allow 4-6 weeks for delivery.
This offer is subject to withdrawal without notice.

ON SALE NOW!

A new realm of romance and passion—the first of Signet's Super Regency novels ... "A superb spellbinder ... captures the heart and soul of the Regency era."—*Romantic Times*

LOVE IN DISGUISE
by
Edith Layton

She was torn between two passionate men—and driven toward one burning dream ...

Miss Susannah Logan felt very fortunate to have not one, but two gentlemen shepherding her through her first London season. The wealthy Warwick Jones, whose pretended scorn for women was matched only by the sensual intensity of his passion for them. The honorable Viscount Julian Hazelton, whose fierce desire for an unobtainable beauty had led him to financial ruin. Each led Susannah on a different path of love and passion toward a decision that threatened to intoxicate her flesh ... and yield her ripe innocence to the one man whose tantalizing nearness she could no longer resist....

Buy them at your local bookstore or use this convenient coupon for ordering.

NEW AMERICAN LIBRARY
P.O. Box 999, Bergenfield, New Jersey 07621

Please send me _____ paperback copies of LOVE IN DISGUISE (0-451-149238) at $3.50 U.S./4.50 Can. (Please add $1.00 per order to cover postage and handling). I enclose check or money order (no cash or C.O.D.'s) or charge my   MasterCard   VISA.

Card #_____

Signature_____

Name_____

Address_____

City _____ State _____ Zip Code _____

⊘ SIGNET REGENCY ROMANCE (0451)

A REALM OF ROMANCE

☐	LORD HARRY'S FOLLY by Catherine Coulter.	(137655—$2.50)
☐	LORD DEVERILL'S HEIR by Catherine Coulter.	(134818—$2.50)
☐	THE REBEL BRIDE by Catherine Coulter.	(138376—$2.50)
☐	THE GENEROUS EARL by Catherine Coulter.	(136187—$2.50)
☐	AN HONORABLE OFFER by Catherine Coulter.	(112091—$2.25)
☐	THE ENCHANTING STRANGER by Barbara Hazard.	(132475—$2.50)
☐	THE CALICO COUNTESS by Barbara Hazard.	(129164—$2.25)
☐	A SURFEIT OF SUITORS by Barbara Hazard.	(138872—$2.50)
☐	THE DISOBEDIENT DAUGHTER by Barbara Hazard.	(138848—$2.50)
☐	THE DREADFUL DUKE by Barbara Hazard.	(139127—$2.50)
☐	THE RAKE'S PROTÉGÉE by Barbara Hazard.	(136160—$2.50)
☐	THE TURNABOUT TWINS by Barbara Hazard.	(142586—$2.50)

Buy them at your local bookstore or use this convenient coupon for ordering.

NEW AMERICAN LIBRABY,
P.O. Box 999, Bergenfield, New Jersey 07621

Please send me the books I have checked above. I am enclosing $_____
(please add $1.00 to this order to cover postage and handling). Send check
or money order—no cash or C.O.D.'s. Prices and numbers subject to change
without notice.

Name _____

Address_____

City_____State_____Zip Code_____
Allow 4-6 weeks for delivery.
This offer is subject to withdrawal without notice.